running
the bases
jennifer kitchen

# running the bases

## definitely not a book about baseball

Paul Kropp

DOUBLEDAY CANADA

LIBRARY AND ARCHIVES CANADA CATALOGUING IN PUBLICATION

Kropp, Paul, 1948–
Running the bases : definitely not a book about baseball / Paul Kropp.

ISBN 0-385-66147-9

I. Title.

PS8571.R772R86 2005     jC813'.54     C2005-902449-6

Cover image: altrendo images / Getty Images
Cover and text design: Leah Springate
Printed and bound in Canada

Published in Canada by
Doubleday Canada, a division of
Random House of Canada Limited

Visit Random House of Canada Limited's website: www.randomhouse.ca

TRANS 10 9 8 7 6 5 4 3 2 1

*To Lori, my wife,*
*my partner and my inspiration*

# contents

# 1

# You Don't Start With a Home Run

"YOU DON'T START with a home run," Jeremy said.

"A what?" I replied.

"You don't start off with some girl jumping in bed with you. You've got to run the bases, you know, the first kiss, the messing around . . . and then you get to home base."

"Oh, home base," I mumbled. A girl named Allison was walking by and had caught my eye. She did a little modelling around town, sometimes appearing in newspaper supplements dressed in revealing lingerie. Today she was dressed in baggy sweats, with no makeup and fly-away hair, but she was still gorgeous.

"And you don't start with somebody like that," Jeremy went on. We both watched Allison disappear in the distance. "You've got to start with somebody in your league," Jeremy told me.

"What league is that?"

"Like maybe peewee. Face it, Alan, you're never going to make it with any of the hot girls around here."

Jeremy and I were in the high-school cafeteria, looking around at the various groups nearby. There was a pattern to the way people sat at the tables. Rich kids sat with rich kids, eating the expensive pizza slices; poor kids sat with poor kids eating their brown-bag lunches; smart kids sat with smart kids, actually talking about math or history; the hot girls sat with the other hot girls; the losers with the losers; and I sat with Jeremy. We were beginning the Alan project—a systematic effort to find a girl for me.

Jeremy was my project manager. At the age of seventeen, I just decided it was time to move on from my dateless, romanceless adolescent life. I decided it was time to abandon my fantasy girls, dream dates and jpegs and actually go out with a real girl.

My friend Jeremy has been going out with girls since grade five, long before I knew him. He tells me that his sex appeal mystifies even himself, but Jeremy deals with it philosophically as a burden he has to carry. I can't understand his success with girls either, since Jeremy isn't particularly good looking and has an unusual amount of spit on his lips most of the time, a trait that gives the general impression that he's drooling. But there's no accounting for the choices of women, I tell myself. Look at André Agassi—and he doesn't even have any hair.

"I think we have to start you at a lower level," Jeremy told me as he scanned the cafeteria. "Maybe Jasmine, over there," he said, pointing to a dark-haired girl sitting by the window. "She's a butterface."

"A what?"

"A butterface. She's got a really hot body, but her face isn't so good."

"Oh, like everything's good but her face," I said. This project of improving my social life was coming with an expanded vocabulary.

"Or maybe Hannah the Honker would go out with you," he said, grinning at me. "With a nose like that, I doubt that she'd have a lot of guys chasing after her."

Hannah had been our classmate since grade seven. I wouldn't have minded a date with Hannah, since at least it would be fun, but the moment didn't seem right to tell this to Jeremy.

"Is that it—a choice of two?" I asked him.

"Okay, how about Maggie over there?" He pointed to a skinny red-haired girl wearing a baggy sweatshirt and jeans. "She's a bit of an ugger with those braces and the glasses and all, but probably about your level."

"My level?" I repeated.

"Actually, she's a cut above your level, but let's ignore that for the moment. You already know her, right?"

I nodded. I had known Maggie McPherson for ten years or so, ever since we had been on the same soccer team when we were six or seven years old. Back then, she was skinny and well coordinated;

I was chunky and more than likely to fall on my face while kicking the ball. Of course, that was a long time ago. These days Maggie is still skinny and she may or may not be coordinated. But she is about the smartest kid at Regis High School, destined for some glittering future if the scholarships come through.

"Maggie might even get off on a nerdy type like you," Jeremy went on. "Besides, I hear she has no social life, so she's probably pretty desperate."

"Desperate is good," I agreed.

"Desperate is essential in your case," Jeremy said. "It's your only chance. As your project manager, I'm advising you to make a play for Maggie. It might just work."

I sighed. With friends like Jeremy, it's possible that I don't need any enemies.

"So what do I do?" I asked him.

"You go up and start with a little chat about something, anything, then you ask her to go to the dance. Pop the question, as it were."

I gave him a look. Jeremy is inclined to use phrases like "as it were" in order to sound like a British lord rather than the pimply-faced high-school student he actually is. Or should I say, we actually are.

"Chat?" I repeated.

"About the weather, or school, or something. It used to be called small talk back in the black-and-white movie days. You know how to talk, don't you?"

At that moment, I wasn't sure whether I remembered how to breathe. Maggie was sitting alone at one of the long tables, reading a book despite the noise and confusion of the cafeteria. She usually had lunch with a couple of other girls, but today she was by herself. It was a golden opportunity to make my move.

"Don't lose your courage, Al," Jeremy told me. "Go for it."

"Right, go for it," I repeated, mostly to myself.

I got up on shaky legs and started in Maggie's direction. I could feel perspiration everywhere—on my forehead, dripping from my armpits, turning my shirt into a soggy mess. I suspect even my ears were dripping with nervous perspiration.

It wasn't that Maggie looked all that intimidating. She sat there in her usual baggy-everything outfit and pink-grey running shoes from some no-name company. She had little round glasses balanced halfway down a button nose. That nose, and most of her cheeks, were dotted with freckles. Her usually frizzy red-blonde hair was pulled back into some kind of half ponytail. And she had a ketchup smear just under her lip.

"Hey, Maggie," I said when I got close. I managed to knock against a couple of empty chairs as I made my way between tables.

She looked up over her glasses and gave me a smile, or maybe it was a wince, I couldn't be sure.

"Mind if I sit down?"

"It's a free country, as the phrase goes," she replied.

I chose to interpret that as a yes. Jeremy had said that I should think positive, think of myself as strong, masculine and desirable. He also told me to exude confidence, but right now all I was exuding was sweat.

"So, nice day, isn't it?" I began.

She looked out the cafeteria windows. "It's cold and it's raining."

I had to think fast. "Yeah, well it's a nice day if you like rain, and I kind of like rain because it's, uh, kind of damp, if you enjoy the damp kind of thing."

*My god,* I thought, *I sound retarded.* She must think I have an IQ of 32. I had to do something to redeem myself—I had to say something interesting, something intelligent, if not brilliant.

Nothing came to mind.

"So what about that math test?" I said. "Wasn't that a killer?" There. Not brilliant, but something that we had in common. Mr. Greer's math test had been on area and volume, something about the number of cucumbers you could plant in a field so-by-so big, given so much space per cucumber, which might be interesting if I were a cucumber farmer but otherwise left my mind reeling.

"I kind of liked it," Maggie replied. "Those problem tests give you a chance to think, you know?"

"Oh, yeah, I liked it too," I lied, knowing I'd be lucky to pass. "Thinking . . . well, thinking is always a good thing."

*Oh no, I'm sounding like an idiot again. I talk like I've never had a thought in my life. Maybe my IQ really* is 32.

"So speaking of thinking," I went on, hoping for a clever segue into the real topic, "I've been thinking about the dance next Friday."

"Oh, *that!*" she said, spitting out the word like the dance was about as appealing as a cockroach scurrying under the fridge. "The Spring Fling thing. What a cheesy name for a dance."

"Yeah, well, I guess," I said, never having thought twice about it. "I was kind of wondering if you were thinking of going."

She actually stopped to look at me through those little glasses of hers. I felt as if she were studying my face, maybe counting the droplets of sweat on my forehead. Naturally, that brought on a new shower of perspiration.

"Maybe," she said with a verbal shrug. "It's mostly a first-year thrill, but I might go if Friday looks kind of void."

*This is hopeless,* I thought. I can't seem to put three words together that make sense and I'm trying to ask out a girl who can use the word *void* in conversation. Why did I let Jeremy push me into this?

"So I was thinking," I said, but then I was aware that I was repeating myself, so I stopped talking and thought about repeating myself and how stupid that was and how stupid I must be to repeat myself except I'm really not that stupid so I must just be nervous but how stupid it was to be nervous because I was just asking her to a dance and the worst she could say was no and so what was the big deal anyhow?

"Hello, Alan," she said suddenly. "Earth to Alan, come in."

"Oh, yeah, sure."

"For a second I thought you were having some kind of seizure, like that guy Simon in *Lord of the Flies.*"

"I was just thinking," I explained.

"Oh, right," she said, and took another bite of her hamburger. The bite made a pickle shoot out of the burger and fall to the table between us. I thought I might try to say something witty about the pickle trajectory, or maybe make some clever literary connection to pickles, but my mind was blank.

It was Maggie who broke the silence. "Oh, I get it," she said. "You want to ask me to the dance!"

"Well, uh, yeah." Now my face was turning red. I was sweating buckets—no, swimming pools—and now I felt like my face was burning up.

"You want to do that whole I'll-pick-you-up-at-seven-and-hold-your-hand-and-kiss-you-goodnight thing, right?" She said this as if the idea just amazed her.

I hadn't let my mind jump so far ahead, certainly not as far as the kiss-you-goodnight thing, but given the pickle bits stuck in her braces and the ketchup on her chin, it didn't seem all that attractive a concept.

Her eyes seemed to widen behind her glasses. "You think I'm so desperate for a date that I'd go out with you!" she went on.

"I never said 'desperate,'" I replied.

"But you were thinking it," she told me. "You were thinking, there's a girl so desperate she'd even go out with Al Macklin. That's what you were thinking, weren't you?"

"No . . . no, I wasn't thinking at all."

"But you said you were thinking, just a couple seconds ago."

"But I wasn't thinking. Or I wasn't thinking about that."

"What were you thinking?"

"I was thinking . . ." and then I forgot what I had been thinking about.

So now we were both stuck in silence. It seemed the whole cafeteria had fallen into a kind of hush, as though everyone was listening in to this pathetic conversation.

"I'll tell you what I'm thinking," said another voice. Maggie and I both looked up. It was Hannah the Honker, standing with a cafeteria tray in her hand. "I'm thinking you should get out of my chair, Alan."

So I got up, looked at Maggie, then looked at Hannah and then looked at the only safe place—at my shoes.

"Well, see ya," I said lamely, and to nobody in particular.

"See ya," Maggie said as I turned away. And that was the last thing I heard, though I swear Hannah used the word *loser* in some kind of sentence just before I was out of earshot.

It was a long, slow walk across the cafeteria. I was sure the eyes of everyone in the room were glued to me, all of them thinking *loser* as my heavy feet trod the floor. I felt like one of those death-row prisoners you see in movies, walking down the cell block to the electric chair while the other inmates pound their metal cups against the bars.

I slumped down beside Jeremy.

"Got shot down, eh?" he said. I guess he could see the whole episode written on my face. "Sometimes they do that," he said brightly. "It's a complex psychological response. See, if she shoots you down, then she bolsters her own self-esteem because (a) you asked her out and (b) she was so superior to your asking her out that she turned you down and (c) . . . well, I can't think of a (c)."

He waited a respectful two seconds before going on. "Did she give you any reasons? Like, was it you personally or the dance generally or has she got somebody to go with or what?"

"Last choice," I mumbled. "The what."

"What?" he repeated.

"It all got twisted up," I explained.

"Well, you can't just give up, Al," he told me. "Now sit back and look confident. That's better. See if you can smile as if going to the dance with that little ugger never even crossed your mind."

"She's not an ugger," I said.

"We can discuss that later. Right now, you've got to smile. People are watching so they need to see confidence, *savoir faire, sang-froid, je ne sais quoi.*"

"What's *sang-froid?*"

"How should I know? I'm studying Spanish." Jeremy had a wonderful self-confidence that I'd always envied. "It just sounds good."

"Yeah, right."

"Don't despair, Al. This was only a first attempt. By the end of the summer, I promise, not only will you be a success with girls"— he leaned forward to deliver the rest in a serious whisper—"but we're going to get you laid."

# 2

# A Surprise at the Dance

"YOU LOOK VERY nice, Alan." That was my mother speaking just before I left for the school dance. Of course her idea of nice was me wearing a sweater without food stains and putting enough gel in my hair that the weird hairs growing at the back didn't spring up.

"Thanks," I mumbled.

I almost agreed with her, for a change. I was having a good-acne and good-hair day, two big pluses. I had picked out a pair of pants that seemed pretty reasonable, a nice button-down shirt, and my least-scuffed pair of Nikes.

"Are you taking anyone to the dance?" She asked this innocently enough, passing by in the upstairs hall while I sprayed on one more layer of deodorant.

My mother feels quite guilty about prying into my life, but of course that doesn't stop her from snooping around as much as she can. I put telltale Scotch tape on my notebooks and dresser drawers, so I know that she checks for homework and looks in my drawers for porn, condoms, booze or dope—the major sins of a teenage guy's life. So far, both my drawers and my life have been remarkably free of sin.

"No, I'm not taking anybody. I'm going with Jeremy."

"He's such a nice boy," she said.

From my mother's point of view, Jeremy was polite, didn't dress too ghetto and always brought her a chocolate on Mother's Day. She thought he was a wonderful kid to have as my best friend. What she didn't know was that Jeremy has more porn on his computer than I have Word files. I suspect that information might change her opinion.

Jeremy wasn't too thrilled about going along with me to the dance. He said that St. Hilda's was having a dance the same night and he was going to go to that dance with some girl named Mona or Monica. Jeremy is always going off to church dances and says he prefers girls from Catholic schools. I think that's funny because Jeremy is Jewish and we both go to a public high school, but he says that the Catholic girls have a touch of class about them, a *je ne sais quoi,* he would say, except that he studied Spanish.

Nonetheless, Jeremy agreed to give up an evening with Mona or Monica to keep me company at the Regis High School Spring Fling. I think he felt guilty about the way Maggie had demolished me in the cafeteria. Or maybe he thought he could get the project back on track by finding somebody for me at the dance.

"Hey, Alan," Jeremy said, walking in our front door after a quick knock. "You're not going like that, are you?"

"What do you mean, 'like that'?"

"I mean, like *that,* like how you're dressed."

"What's wrong with how I'm dressed?" I shot back. "My mother said I looked fine."

"That should have been your first clue, Al," he said in a whisper. "When your mother thinks you look good, you really look like a total reject. It's the rule. Never listen to your mom on matters of clothing, romance or advanced math."

"Oh," I replied.

"You look like you're going to McDonald's for the Happy Meal. I mean, those shoes have got to go. You can't dance in those. And the shirt? Have you ever seen anybody on a music video wearing a button-down shirt? Frankly, Al, you can't do much about your face or your hopeless hair, but you can at least pick some decent clothes. Let's go see what's in your closet."

It took a good half-hour for Jeremy to re-dress me for the dance. This time, I was mostly in black: black shoes, black pants, black T with a wonky Hawaiian shirt that my uncle had brought back from Oahu, and a black necklace that Jeremy found in my mom's room.

"A necklace?" I said.

"It means you're not worried about dressing like a girl. It means you're sexually confident."

"But what if I'm not."

"Then fake it. Remember, Al, this is part of a long-term project. Don't lose sight of the goal."

It was easy to lose sight of everything when I stared at myself in the mirror. Together, we looked like the two Men in Black, except he wasn't Will Smith and I wasn't Tommy Lee Jones, even after we put on the sunglasses.

"Now that's cool," Jeremy said.

"I look just like you," I told him.

"That's what I said, Al, you look cool. Now let's go."

The two of us walked to school, avoiding the demeaning offer of a ride from my mom. It didn't matter how cool you dressed if you got out of the family van for a school dance. "Your entrance," Jeremy told me, "is key. Imagine you're going into the party scene in *La Traviata*." Jeremy's father is into opera, so he can talk about things like that.

Our actual entrance to the school dance didn't quite measure up to an operatic standard. Old Mr. Tarkington, the VP, smiled at the two of us and mumbled something unintelligible; the official rent-a-cop looked at me as if I had a mickey of whisky hidden in my shirt; and the breathless student council social convenor took our tickets without looking up or even once batting her gorgeous blue eyes. When we walked into the dance, I found myself quite blind in the darkened gym. It turned out that I couldn't see much of anything wearing the sunglasses, so I pushed them down on my nose and looked out over their lenses.

Elegant it was not. You can flash some strobe lights in a school gym, you can set up big video screens under the basketball nets, but you still can't eliminate the smell of fifty years of dirty socks and sweaty underarms. I wondered if *La Traviata* had ever been performed in a school gym.

"Hey, dude," I heard. It was the voice of Leroy Anderson, a kid we'd called Scrooge ever since a monumental production of

A *Christmas Carol* back in grade three. Leroy was maybe the first black Scrooge ever, and he pulled off the role so brilliantly that the nickname stuck.

"Hey, guy," I replied. All I could see through the sunglasses were his smiling teeth.

"You look cool," he said.

"Thanks," I replied. I figured that approval from Scrooge was probably worth more than a few kind words from my mother.

"Hey, Scrooge," Jeremy piped up, "any babes around here?"

"The usual," he reported. "Marci came with Adrienne, but they're just here to dance. Joanna brought a date, Allison has five guys hanging off her, Nikki's wearing a top so tight you could bounce a quarter off it, and that's about it except for the baby chicks."

The baby chicks were the girls in their first year of high school. These were the minor niners who giggled whenever you said anything, dressed like J. Lo but without her physical assets, and tended to smell like a mix of bubble gum and cheap perfume. We, of course, were two years older and therefore much more sophisticated.

"Alan's looking for a girl," Jeremy volunteered.

"Anybody in particular?" Scrooge asked.

"Nah, he'll settle for anything older than a baby chick. Maybe Naomi?"

"She came with Rod," Scrooge said, "so there's no way."

"Jen Beecroft?"

"Haven't seen her."

I thought it was time to offer my own suggestion. "How about Allison?"

I could see their eyes, staring at me, even through the sunglasses. I had an idea of the look on their faces.

"Get real, Alan," Scrooge told me. "She's the closest thing we have to a goddess here, and you just wouldn't make the cut. And the way she spreads gossip—Al, you'd be the laughingstock of the school in no time." He took a moment to reflect, and then grinned at me. "I mean, even *I* don't have a chance with Allison."

I guess that put me in my place. Scrooge pretty much had his pick of the girls in our school. He was cool, funny, smart, talented and black—a pretty devastating combination in a town of 150,000 that had very few black guys, and none who were cool, funny, smart and talented except Scrooge himself.

In comparison, I was klutzy, dull, dim-witted, unfocussed and pimpled. If Scrooge couldn't get anywhere with Allison Mackenzie, I couldn't even get in her vicinity.

"Let's go look around," Jeremy said to Scrooge. I think he was purposely excluding me. "We'll go scouting and see if there's anybody in your league, Al."

So I was left standing there, in a league of my own.

This dance seemed to be more successful than the previous student council event, which is to say that a few kids actually were dancing. By and large, the first-year kids propped up the walls on two sides—boys on one, girls on the other—the second-year kids hung around the snack bar, and the third-year kids like us tried to stand around and look cool. Fourth-year kids didn't come to these dances, or they came drunk and the rent-a-cop had to usher them out.

I was just standing there, staring at the world through my dark glasses, when Maggie came up beside me.

"Hey, I'm sorry," she said.

"What's that?" I replied. I thought she'd said "I'm slurpy."

"I'm sorry about what I said last week. When you asked me to the dance. I really didn't mean to be mean. Sometimes I get like that, kind of bristly and obnoxious."

"No problem," I replied, looking at her over my shades. Maggie looked kind of good in the coloured lights. She was wearing an iridescent top that caught the light and a pair of low-slung pants that showed a nice bit of skin. There seemed to be some sparkles on her cheeks, which I took to be makeup rather than freckles. And she had taken off her glasses, but I guess she had to squint to see much.

"I figured out later that Jeremy must have put you up to it," she said.

"Up to what?"

"Asking me to the dance."

"Well, he kind of encouraged me. He's my project manager."

"A project manager?" she asked.

"Yeah, or maybe a personal trainer. He's trying to help me get a date . . . I mean, a date with you."

"So I'm like the five-pound barbells that you lift until you get in shape," Maggie suggested. "Then you go on to the heavier weights, like Nikki or Allison."

"No, not like that," I said. "I mean, I like you, kind of, and I just thought you might want to go to the dance, that's all. But you're already here, so it's kind of a moot point."

*Moot point!* I thought to myself. Had I actually said *moot point* in conversation? I'm not even sure I know what *moot point* means.

"Well, I'm sorry," she said, turning away from me. "I didn't mean to be the way that I was. It's just that I'm not ready for this whole dating thing. So I guess I should have said that instead of doing a number on you."

I nodded. We were both quiet for a second while Céline Dion sang something loud and romantic. I can never hear her voice without thinking of all those bodies floating in the water after the *Titanic* sank.

I listened to the music, taking surreptitious peeks at Maggie from the corner of my eye. She seemed to be thinking about something, biting her lip periodically, then finally nodding her head as if she'd made up her mind.

"Looks like your project buddies are back," Maggie said as Jeremy and Scrooge came up.

"Hi, Maggie," Jeremy replied, not missing a beat. "What's this about a project?"

"Alan says you're his project manager in romance, kind of a dating coach."

"Did you say that?" Jeremy asked accusingly.

"Well, not exactly," I mumbled.

Maggie squinted at the two of us. "All I can say is, God help Alan if he's looking to you for advice on girls. You wouldn't know how to come on to a girl if she had both arms wrapped around your neck and was sticking her tongue in your ear."

"Whooo!" Scrooge broke in. "That one came in low and hard!"

Maggie didn't stop. "Alan needs some *good* advice if he wants to start going out with a decent girl. And the best place to get that advice is from . . . a girl."

"Like who?" Scrooge asked.

"Like me," Maggie went on. "Good advice. Reasonable rates. Good connections. If I can't get Alan half a dozen dates in the next couple of months, nobody can."

"Well, we had a little bit more in mind," Jeremy replied. The spit on his lips seemed to glow in the dark, a none-too-pleasant effect.

"I figured," Maggie went on, "but I can't guarantee that. Listen, Alan," she said, turning to me, "if you want me to help on this project, I will. We can start tonight laying out a plan. Meet me at Starbucks after the dance." Then she turned to Jeremy. "That is, if your current project manager will let you stay up that late."

# 3

## Project Costs Escalate

IT WASN'T THAT late when we left for Starbucks. School dances always end at eleven o'clock for some reason, maybe because "Stairway to Heaven" takes forever to play so they have to start it at ten thirty. Actually, the Spring Fling had ended for me even before it began. I didn't even dance, since there was no sense making a fool of myself by asking one of the baby chicks, and the older girls weren't looking particularly friendly.

So there we sat in Starbucks with our grande cappuccinos: danceless me, irritated Jeremy and way-cool Scrooge.

"This is stupid," Jeremy said as he sipped his double frappuccino.

"This is a hoot," Scrooge replied, using one of those seventies terms he gets from his mother.

"This gives me a chance," I told them, gritting my teeth.

Jeremy shot me an angry glance over his grande cup. "Listen, Alan, I already offered to tell you anything you want to know about girls."

"Yeah, what do you know?" Scrooge asked. Scrooge could get away with that because, whenever he called you a BS artist, he did it with this enormous grin on his face.

"I know plenty," Jeremy shot back. "I've been out with more girls than . . . well, maybe not you, Scrooge, but more than most of the guys at school. I know all their secrets, all their little turn-ons. I know all the tricks that'll get Alan laid."

"You ever got laid?" Scrooge asked.

"Yeah," Jeremy said, sticking out his chin. "More times than I can count."

Scrooge laughed. "You are so full of it."

"Shhh," I told them both. "She's here."

We all looked as Maggie came in the door. She nodded to us and got in the lineup for her coffee. Scrooge began grumbling because Allison hadn't come with her, so now I understood his real agenda. Jeremy kept making nasty comments about Maggie and her general lack of style, not to mention her obnoxious attitude. I kept my mouth shut. After all, Maggie's offer of advice had come to me, not to them. They were only here because I needed some moral support.

"I see you brought your crew," Maggie said, sitting down across from me.

"Yeah, well . . ."

"That's the first thing we've got to fix, Alan. If you're going to start moving in on girls, you've got to do it by yourself. This wolf-pack thing just won't work."

"Hey, we're not a wolf pack," Scrooge said. "We're a support group for our buddy here. We give him our solidarity and emotional backup, not to mention the benefit of our wisdom and experience. And by the way, where's Allison?"

"See, you just proved my point. Scrooge, why don't you go prowl the streets and see if you can find her. Failing that, there's a moon you can howl at."

"Whoa!" Scrooge told her. "I can tell when I'm not wanted. C'mon, Jeremy, I think this girl wants to be *alone* with our friend."

"Whooo, pretty romantic," Jeremy joined in. "Nobody told us this was going to be a *private* conversation." He got up out of his chair and looked at me with a superior smile on his face. "Looks like you've got to wrestle this barracuda all by yourself, Al. Lots of luck."

Laughing to each other, my friends headed for the door. I stared at my coffee cup.

"So juvenile," Maggie grumbled.

"Yeah, I guess."

"So listen, Alan, I'm not billing you by the minute or anything, but we might as well get to the point. Just what is it that you want?"

That was a tough one. It was one of those questions that you can't just fire back something easy, your basic one-line zinger that you see on sitcoms all the time.

*What did I want?* Well, I wanted to go out with a girl. No, I wanted a girl to like me, and I wanted to make out and I wanted to have sex. At least, I think I wanted to have sex, but I wasn't really one hundred percent sure about that. After all, sex comes with all sorts of complications, so really I just wanted to make out. But what's the point of making out unless you've got some hope of going all the way, so maybe I really did want sex.

In a second or two, I thought about all those things, except not as clearly, and mostly in pictures rather than words. I often think in pictures, like a very fast dream playing through my brain, and then the words come later. So what I saw was me on a date with Nikki, and me kissing Allison, who was dressed only in lingerie, and me making out with Sarah Michelle Gellar, and a dozen other images— some of them unrepeatable—that went zooming across my mental computer screen.

What I finally said is, "I'm not sure."

"Oh, come on," Maggie replied, shaking her head. "You didn't ask me to the dance because you weren't sure. You had to have some idea about some kind of objective. I mean, even your friends know what they want. Scrooge wants to make a play for Allison just to add to his girl collection and Jeremy wants to get more material for his fantasy life."

"No, Jeremy goes out a lot, but not with girls from our school," I said.

She snorted. "Yeah, right. But the question remains, what do *you* want? Would it be easier if I made it multiple choice?"

"Yeah, that would be good," I said, breathing a little more easily. I'm good at multiple choice; it's the essay questions that kill me.

"Okay, so here's the possible answers," she said, licking some coffee off her bottom lip.

"Ready."

"You want to (a) go out on a date to prove you're normal and not a homosexual, (b) go out with a girl because you've seen it on TV and it looks cool, (c) start a relationship with a girl so you can make out, or (d) you want to get laid."

"Can I pick more than one?"

"No, you have to pick the best answer, just like on Greer's math tests. It may not be the right answer, but the best answer of the ones given."

I suddenly felt very warm, as if the Starbucks staff had chosen that moment to pump up the heat. "Well, uh, I'm seventeen now and I think, you know, it's about time I had a relationship, you know, a serious relationship . . ."

I was in the middle of this long and complex answer, an answer that I thought would be both forthright and politically correct, an answer that would get Maggie on my side and pave the way for a brilliant social life for the rest of the school year if not the rest of my life, but something short-circuited in my brain and the big answer stopped cold. Then, from somewhere at the back of my brain, another voice took over. "I . . . uh, I pick (d)."

*Ohmygod,* I thought. I've just told a girl, an actual girl, that what I really want to do is get laid. She'll think I'm a pig. She might hit me. She might tell all her friends.

Maggie didn't do any of those things. "Well, at least you're honest," she said. "I thought I was going to have to sit here for an hour while you went through some convoluted BS about wanting a deep and meaningful relationship. I mean, at seventeen who's looking for deep and meaningful?"

"Uh, right," I said. I believe I gulped rather loudly, perhaps in relief, perhaps in gratitude.

"I personally favour shallow and meaningless, at least for now," she went on.

"I thought you didn't . . ."

"Oh, I don't. I'm speaking theoretically here," Maggie said, not missing a beat. "And *my* social life is not the issue here, it's yours we're working on. With a little help, Alan, I think you'll get laid by summer vacation, if not sooner."

"How?"

"With my help," she replied.

"You're just volunteering to help me?" I think my eyes were as big as a grande coffee lid.

"Yeah, for a small fee."

"A fee!" I shrieked. "I have to pay to get advice? At least Jeremy is helping me out for free."

"Look, Alan, nobody these days does anything out of the good-ness of their hearts," Maggie said. "Even the school volunteer pro-gram is a graduation requirement, and it looks good when you're applying to universities. Personal generosity was something from the Kennedy era, like the last century." Maggie was putting this for-ward in a very matter-of-fact way, like a sales pitch. "And I'm going to give you a good deal on this: a small retainer, project costs and basic fees for service."

"A small retainer . . ."

"Yeah, I think fifty dollars should handle it," she said. "But you didn't let me finish. I will guarantee results."

"A guarantee?" I said. My mouth had already dropped open so the words came out a little funny.

"Yeah, a money-back guarantee. You'll get laid by summer vaca-tion or your money is refunded, no questions asked." Maggie stared at me, maybe trying to focus since I knew she couldn't see without her glasses.

"You're serious?" I said.

"Dead serious," she replied. "Is it a deal, Al, or do you need time to think about it? I suggest you not check with your current project manager, since he won't give you an unbiased view. It's your call: free advice from a loser or good advice from someone who can give you the secrets of success."

This was starting to sound like an infomercial. Secrets of suc-cess? Doesn't everyone want the secrets of success?

"Well, I've probably got fifty bucks I could spare," I said. I had a few hundred dollars sitting in the bank, thanks to gifts from Aunt Betty and a few odd jobs in the neighbourhood. And for summer I had lined up a job at Dairy Queen, so I could spare a little money for this.

"Then we've got a deal," Maggie concluded. "Bring the cash to lunch on Monday and I'll give you your starting instructions and the name of your first target girl. Fair enough?"

"Yeah, I guess," I mumbled.

"And Al, in the meanwhile, try to dress a little better. That Men in Black look is so out of it."

# 4

# The Agreement

WHAT IS FIFTY BUCKS? I asked myself. Maybe ten movie
rentals, or the price of a decent dinner out. I mean, you can spend
fifty dollars on a *book!* So I got the cash from the bank machine and
met Maggie in the cafeteria on Monday.

"You brought the retainer?" she asked.

"Yeah," I said, pulling the envelope out of my math book.

"Good," she said, smiling her silvery smile. Maggie had her
glasses back on and was dressed in a jacket that made her look like
a lawyer-in-training. "I've selected the start-up girl for you."

"Who?"

"Not so fast," Maggie replied. "There are some terms and conditions to this project, so we'd better sign off on those."

I was starting to sweat. This was turning out to be much more
serious than I ever imagined.

"Here's the agreement, fee schedule and guarantee," Maggie
said, pushing a sheet of paper forward.

"You ever think of becoming a lawyer?" I asked.

"Only every other day," she replied, deadpan. "Just read it over
and make sure it's acceptable."

Agreement between Alan Macklin (hereafter referred to as "the Dater") and Maggie McPherson (hereafter referred to as "the Project Manager")

Project: Alan
Dated: March 8

*(i) Whereas:* The Dater is desirous of improving his social life and learning to date girls in a successful manner;

And the Dater has an Ultimate Goal, herewith defined as sexual intimacy with a girl, this intimacy to be non-commercial in nature and the culmination of his dating activity;

And the Dater acknowledges that both his experience and expertise is limited in this endeavour so he recognizes his need for advice and counsel.

*(ii) It is agreed that:* The Project Manager will offer advice and counsel to the Dater with the aim of helping him to achieve his goals;

The Project Manager will work confidentially on the Dater's behalf;

The Project Manager will bill the Dater monthly according to the following fee schedule:

- memos of advice, 50 cents per word
- meetings for advice, $10 per half-hour
- successful first-date arrangements, $25
- follow-up dates, $5 per date
- successful achievement of Ultimate Goal, $100

*(iii) Retainer:* The Dater agrees to pay a $50 retainer against such future billings as might be involved in the project. This retainer is not returnable in the event of cancellation.

*(iv) Expenses:* The Dater agrees to reimburse the Project Manager for such expenses as are deemed necessary to complete the duties listed in clause ii, above.

*(v) Billing:* The Project Manager will bill the Dater monthly for services rendered, such bills to be itemized.

*(vi)* **Cancellation:** This agreement may be cancelled by either party on receipt of two days' notice, in writing. Following cancellation, a full and final billing will be delivered by the Project Manager to the Dater.

*(vii)* **Warranty:** The Project Manager guarantees that the Dater will achieve his Ultimate Goal before June 30, or all monies received, with the exception of the retainer and expenses, will be returned at the request of the Dater.

*(viii)* **Expiry:** This agreement expires as of July 1, unless an extension is agreed upon by both parties.

"I tried to keep the language simple," Maggie said.

"So I end up paying you five dollars a date, like forever?"

"No, you pay $25 for the first date, then five dollars for each subsequent date until the agreement expires," Maggie explained. "Getting you ready for the first date is a lot more work for me. Besides, a date itself will cost you a lot more than five bucks, even going to a movie."

"You didn't define 'date,'" I pointed out.

"There's got to be some trust in a relationship like this," Maggie replied. "We both know what a date is. And I won't know for sure if you achieve your Ultimate Goal, though I suspect I'll hear rumours about it. This just sets down the initial terms and conditions, to avoid problems later on."

"Is your father a lawyer?"

"No, a school custodian. I'm going to be the lawyer. Now are you ready to sign off and give me the money, or am I wasting my time here?"

I looked at the agreement and did a quick calculation in my head. I'd be spending at least a hundred dollars on Maggie's advice, but that's about the same as an hour with a decent psychiatrist. Besides, this came with a guarantee. What shrink could ever guarantee what I wanted?

So I signed two copies of Maggie's agreement, one for me, one for her, then handed over the envelope. I was pleased to see that she didn't count the bills right in the middle of the cafeteria. As she had said, trust would be an important part of this whole project.

"So what girl did you pick?" I asked.

"Your target girl is Melissa Halvorsen."

"Isn't she a little young?"

"So?" Maggie's thin eyebrows lifted up as she looked back at me. "Melissa's bright. She can talk about something besides makeup and movie stars. And her standards aren't too high. I know she was going out with Josh Weisbaum last year, and he's hardly god's gift."

It all went by so quickly that I didn't even catch the implied insult in her last sentence.

"Well, I guess she'd be good," I said. I mean, I had to say something.

"But I better be clear on this," Maggie went on. "I'm not saying that Mel is easy. She's young, so I don't think you'll get to your Ultimate Goal with her, but you have to start somewhere. Call it a practice relationship. It'll give you a chance to learn how to hold hands, say nice things about her hair and learn how to kiss."

"I can kiss," I said defensively.

Maggie snorted. "Yeah, every guy thinks he knows how to kiss. You just don't hear what the girls are saying on the other side. I tell you, Alan, you guys have a lot to learn."

"And you're going to help me?" I asked.

"All the way," she said brightly. "That's what you're paying me for. I'll start nosing around to see if there's a millivolt of interest."

"A millivolt?"

"You never know, maybe there's even a full volt, maybe your love potential is up to a flashlight battery."

I just looked at her, stunned.

"What I mean is, I'll tell a couple of Mel's friends that you're interested and see what I hear back. Maybe she's got a vague interest in you; maybe not. I've got to check out the potential before you make a fool of yourself again. I mean, you didn't just think that you were going to walk up to Mel and ask her out, did you?"

"Well, kind of."

"It doesn't work like that, Al. It's like fishing. You have to bait the hook, then wait to see if there are nibbles, and then wait until the fish bites. You don't just take a club and smash the fish on its head."

*Dating and fishing.* I'd never seen the connection.

"Leave it with me and I'll get back to you in a couple of days."

# 5

## Target Number One

I BEGAN CHECKING out Melissa Halvorsen in the halls. Big shoulders, big hair, big everything . . . but nicely assembled, as Jeremy put it. Since she was a year younger than me, she wasn't in any of my classes. But I knew her older brother, one of the stars of the Regis football team, and I knew a little about Melissa, too. She played a strange sport called field hockey, at which she was apparently quite good. She was said to be a decent student, but not exceptional, with more talent in phys. ed. than English. In school she had no reputation, one way or another, except that she'd wasted a year of her life going out with Josh Weisbaum, who was a notorious jerk. But Mel was young, as Maggie had pointed out, and deserved to be forgiven for such poor judgment.

Just in case Mel was checking *me* out, I began dressing a little better for school. Less of my usual pulled-out-T-shirt-dangling-sideways look and more of the put-together, semi-cool look. Or so I thought.

"Aren't those pants a little low?" my mother asked.

"It's the style, Ma," I told her.

"And they're all baggy around your shoes. You might trip and fall over."

"I'll be careful, Ma."

A man has to take risks in the name of style. It sounded like a saying worthy of Confucius, but I didn't share it with my mother. Clothes weren't my main concern; Mel Halvorsen was.

For a week, nothing happened. No eye contact. No word from Maggie. Nothing—except continuing ridicule from my friend Jeremy.

"You look like a jerk, man!" Jeremy would say. "Not even Hannah the Honker would go out with somebody like you." Or later, "Why are you wasting time with a fat little chick like Mel? I could find you a better girl at St. Hilda's, no problem."

I hadn't fully explained to Jeremy my arrangement with Maggie. I was suffering enough from his nasty comments without giving him more ammunition.

As March dragged on, I was starting to lose patience. I figured Maggie had abandoned Project Alan, or that my Ultimate Goal was now the laughingstock of every girl in school. What's worse, I was in one of my bad-zit phases. Not only were there the usual dozen zits on both cheeks, but I had a real monster on my nose. I was Rudolf, and it wasn't even Christmas.

In math class, I was thinking about that monster zit when Maggie zoomed in. "See me after school, at the library," she whispered. Then the ever-vigilant Mr. Greer forced us all into zombie-style silence.

I was a little nervous as I waited around the library for Maggie to show up. Our library is not particularly a hot spot after school— there were some kids working on projects, a couple of kids who actually play chess, a few kids surfing for a project or else trying to find a way around the anti-porn software. Still, it was sunny and reasonably quiet. A good place to lay out a plan.

Maggie came storming in, looking at her watch even as she came through the door. She had to squint to see because she wasn't wearing her glasses again. "Okay, we've got to be quick. I've got a ride home in about fifteen minutes."

"Right," I said. "So what's the story?"

"Mel's interested, vaguely, in you. Not *hugely* interested, but not definitely put off by the concept. I planted the usual rumours that you had the hots for her, and after a few giggles she didn't seem to object. At least, those are the reports."

I felt like a soldier preparing for battle. General Maggie had seen reports from the scouts, indicating favourable enemy positions. Now it was a matter of preparing for the initial skirmish. *Lieutenant Alan reporting, sir!*

"So tomorrow you're going to invite her out for coffee."

*Yes, sir!* I almost said. "When?"

"After school for the invite. She'll have to lie and say she's busy if you ask her to go out right away, so make it the next day—that's Thursday."

*Yes, sir!* "And then?"

"She'll say yes, unless you . . ." Suddenly she focussed on my nose. "Jeez, that's a mean zit."

I probably turned a bit red, though not as red as the zit itself.

"Anyway, the zit will have cleared by tomorrow," Maggie went on. I think she felt a little bad about embarrassing me. "So when you go for coffee, just chat a little, back and forth, and then ask her to a movie on the weekend."

"Chat a little?" I asked.

"Yeah, like small talk. About the weather, or school, or something."

I had heard this advice once before. "Look, I'm not so good at small talk."

"So what do you want me to do? Give you a list of things to talk about?" Maggie shot me an incredulous though unfocussed look, her thin eyebrows going way up high.

"Yeah, that would be good," I said.

"Jeez, we've got a long way to go on this, Al. Okay, I'll scribble down some ideas for you. I'll get them to you in math tomorrow. Just remember, there's a small fee for each memo."

"I can handle it."

"Good," she said, looking at the library door. "Anyhow, I've got to run."

"Big date?" I asked, grinning stupidly. From what I heard, Maggie had never been out on a date with anyone.

Maggie frowned at me, screwing up her mouth in a funny way. "Ride home. Braden's got the car today." She raced out of the library so fast that I didn't have time to respond.

Braden? Not Braden Boyce, Mr. B.B. himself, the all-star senior who had to fight off girls with a stick. Couldn't possibly be *that* Braden.

~~~

By the following day, as Maggie predicted, my monster zit was down to ordinary zit size. On the other hand, I was all pumped up. Mel Halvorsen was already interested in me. She already knew I liked her and hadn't fallen down laughing or begun to vomit. There was hope.

All I needed were those ideas on small talk. Our class had a test scheduled for math that afternoon, but that wouldn't have been a problem if Maggie hadn't come in late. Everyone else was already seated when Maggie burst through the door, breathless, with some excuse about phys. ed. running overtime.

Mr. Greer was not amused. Mr. Greer was the kind of teacher who was *never* amused. We sometimes called him "he-who-cannot-smile" and speculated about why he might be unwilling to show his teeth. A century ago, we figured, Mr. Greer would be the kind of teacher who would use a strap to beat math concepts into students' heads. Now he used wicked tests and blistering sarcasm, perhaps with equal effect.

Still, Maggie was his favourite student and she had a decent excuse to be late, so there wasn't much that he could say when she raced to her desk.

There was nothing he could say until she dropped the list on my desk.

"Margaret," Mr. Greer told her, "we don't allow cheat sheets in this room."

"Yes, sir," she said, blushing. "I know that."

"So what did you just leave on Alan's desk?"

"Some notes, sir. On a project . . . for another class. Nothing that will help him on the test. It's not a cheat sheet."

"Well suppose you bring these 'notes' to me," he said, his voice heavy with sarcasm, "and I'll be the judge."

Maggie dutifully picked up her memo to me and took it to the teacher.

"Thank you, Miss McPherson. Alan can pick these up after class if they are what you say they are."

The rest of the class followed this exchange with mild curiosity. Maggie had no reason to give me—of all people—a cheat sheet. She'd risk failing and so would I. So there were a couple of giggles in the class as she took her "notes" to Mr. Greer. And a bit of wonder, too.

It was probably ten minutes into the test that Mr. Greer finished his up-and-down-the-aisles inspection of the class. Obviously there were no other cheat sheets either in paper or scribbled on visible human flesh. The only suspicious document was waiting up on his desk.

I was halfway into some mind-numbing trig problem when Mr. Greer picked up Maggie's notes. He began reading. Then he began smiling. And finally he started to laugh. He laughed so hard he had to say "excuse me" to the kids in the first row.

I turned red in the face. So did Maggie. *Please, please,* I prayed, *don't let him read it out loud. Anything but that, dear Lord.*

The Lord answered my prayer, or else the test ran long and took up the entire period, whatever. Mr. Greer did not read Maggie's list aloud, but that did not stop him from grinning at the whole class as we marched out.

"Alan, just wait up until everyone is out, please," he said.

So I stood there, looking at my feet, as everyone in class looked at me and the ominous piece of paper in Mr. Greer's hands.

When the others had left, Maggie at the end of the file, I had to wait another ten seconds or so in terrible silence. They were very long seconds. They were seconds when you could hear the second hand click ahead on the clock. Finally Mr. Greer handed me Maggie's notes and nodded.

"This *is* a cheat sheet, Alan," he said, "but not for math." He paused for a second. "Good luck, my boy. From the look of this, you'll need it."

## PROJECT: ALAN
Instruction set 1

Your immediate objective is to get a date, Alan. Your long-
term objectives probably include kissing, making out and
getting laid, but stick to your immediate objective for now.
Arrange for coffee tomorrow, then follow these instructions.

### What to talk about:
1. Her. No topic will be more fascinating to Mel Halvorsen than
   herself. Admire her hair, her eyes, her brains, her charm, her
   wit. Girls love praise and admiration. Lay it on thick.
2. Her interests. Find out something about field hockey. Talk
   about it. I hear she watches her brother's football games—
   ask her about them.
3. Her concerns, thoughts, etc. Since she's only sixteen, it's
   likely that Mel doesn't have many thoughts . . . but admire
   whatever she puts forward.

Alan, you'll notice that there's no room in the list above for
YOUR interests. Therefore, do not talk about video games,
your favourite TV shows, your problems in school or your
jerky friends. Nobody cares.

### Do's
1. Look at her eyes. Keep your eyes up there, buddy.
2. Use sucky phrases like "Gosh, that's a really interesting idea,"
   or "How do you keep your hair so perfect all the time?" Resist
   the natural urge to vomit as you spew these lies.
3. Be funny. Girls love a guy who can make them laugh. Find
   a joke on the Internet (a clean one), memorize it and tell it.
4. Be confident. Pretend you've done this before. Don't admit
   that you've never had a date or been within kissing distance
   of a girl.

5. Stick to your immediate goal. You want a date, period. A movie is quick and cheap. If you took her to dinner, you'd have to listen to her for an hour or so and that could be more than anyone could stand.

**Don'ts**
1. Don't look at her breasts, legs or navel (even if it's showing). As I said, keep your eyes up there, buddy.
2. Don't talk or brag much about yourself. She'll be bored with your life and annoyed by your bragging. Humble is good.
3. Don't be a wimp. Confidence should rule the day. Take charge, but don't be bossy.
4. Don't badmouth anyone. (They might be her friends, you never know.)
5. Don't give up. She may say no about tomorrow but be okay for next week. If she's unsure, tell her you'll call. Pretend that you're crazy about her and you just won't give up. Girls love a lovesick guy, unless he gets too lovey or too sicky.

Further instructions will follow. Good luck.

I folded that paper neatly and put it in my pocket. It made me feel good—a whole set of instructions on how to get started with Mel Halvorsen. Maggie had done her job and now I was ready, ready to take on anything.

I found Mel at her locker at the end of the day. She was alone. I took a deep breath and got ready: confident, funny, eyes up, think of the goal, don't give up. Got it. Chest out. Step up and do it.

"Hey, Mel," I said. *Confident. Assured.*

"Hi, Alan."

Now for the opening line I had so carefully prepared. "I was hoping to see you at the dance last week. I've heard you're a really great dancer." *Eyes on her eyes. Smile. Don't blink. Lay it on thick.*

"Oh, thanks, I . . . well, I don't know. I just didn't go."

"Well, I was disappointed. The only reason I went was to see you." *This is a blatant lie, but I mustn't twitch or make a face. Resist the urge to vomit.*

"Oh," she said. I believe she was blushing. Was it possible that she was more nervous than I was?

"So I was wondering if you'd like to go out for coffee after school tomorrow. I'd meet you here and we could just walk over." *That's it, cool and straightforward.*

"Oh, tomorrow, well, I can't," she said, her voice low.

*Uh-oh,* I told myself. For a second I lost eye contact, but then I caught myself. *Don't give up,* Maggie had written.

"So Friday," I suggested. *Be ready,* I told myself. *If it's no, be ready.*

"Oh, Friday would be great. I'd love to."

Was that a smile on her face? Was she actually happy that I had asked her out? Were those perfect teeth and those wonderful lips smiling just for me?

Damn right they were!

# 6

# Achieving Goal One

"THAT'S A PRETTY stupid list," Jeremy said after I let him read Maggie's instructions. I told him that Maggie was just helping me out, as a friend. But Jeremy was unimpressed. "Where's all the stuff about being smooth and masculine and way cool? I mean, how is all this going to get you laid?"

"We're just going for coffee," I told him. "My goal is a date, not a home run. Stick to the goal, that's point number five. Date first, more stuff later."

"I tell you, Al, that's not my style. You've got to move in fast and smooth. A little sexy talk, a touch, a squeeze, a kiss and then some tongue. Hot guys seize the advantage and get laid. Nice guys end up stuck with Hannah the Honker or whipping their own pizoozi."

"We're just going for coffee," I repeated.

He sighed. "Well, if it goes nowhere, I gave you my best advice."

The trouble with Jeremy is that he's got too much experience. Maybe if you've gone out with a dozen girls you can just move in and have them panting for you in a couple of minutes. But I hadn't been out with a dozen girls, not even a couple, not even one. This was date *numero uno,* and it wasn't even a date; it was just coffee. It was really a pre-date. The overture to a date, as our music teacher might say.

"You look good, Al," Maggie told me.

I looked up at her and practised. *Keep your eyes on her eyes,* I reminded myself. I noticed that Maggie was once again without glasses.

"Uh, so do you," I replied.

"Pretty good," she told me. "A little faster with the compliment, though, and maybe some enthusiasm? But I like the eye contact. Remember, a little more praise would be good. Can't have too many compliments."

"Well, you look great Maggie," I told her, smiling just a little. "Your eyes are so sparkling today that it's hard for me to concentrate."

"I like that. A little bit of insincerity always helps."

"Well, it's true," I said, dropping the pose and coming back to reality. "You give up your glasses, or what?" Maggie had been wearing glasses for as long as I could remember. They had come in various sizes, shapes and colours.

"Got contacts," she said, blushing just a little. "I figured if hot guys like you were going to start coming on to me, I might as well try to look like a sex kitten."

I'm not sure that Maggie would fulfill most definitions of *sex kitten*. She was a little too skinny and a little too boyish and had a few too many freckles on her cheeks. But she was cute in a funny kind of way.

"Well, you do look great," I said.

"And you, too, buddy. Now go out there, keep your eyes on her eyes. Just listen to her as if she were the most fascinating person on the planet and you'll get your date. I've got your next set of instructions just about ready."

"More instructions?"

"I've got faith in you, Al, but not that much faith."

With that vote of confidence, I got ready to meet Mel. Before last class I took off for the bathroom, zapped my mouth with breath freshener, took another swipe at my armpits with deodorant and checked the remaining zits on my face for threatened eruptions. All systems were go.

So I felt semi-confident when I met Melissa at her locker. She was looking pretty hot, with a tight top that attracted far more than the passing glance I was allowed to give it, a decent chunk of midriff looking very bare indeed and a pair of jeans that might have been spray-painted on.

"Hi there," I said, my eyes trained on her face. "You look great. I've been looking forward to this all day."

"Well, thanks," she said. "Me too." Then she giggled. I hadn't realized that she was a giggler, but in grade ten I guess all the girls were gigglers.

"Ready for a frappuccino?" I asked. It sounded oh, so suave.

"How about a latte?" she replied.

"Anything for you, Mel," I told her as we headed down the hall. She had her books pulled up against her breasts in that way girls always do, but I didn't look. I kept my eyes up, up, up.

"Tell me, have you always liked lattes, or is this something new?"

"Well, I had my first one in, like, grade seven," she began, and then the words began to pour forth. Not only was Mel a giggler, she was a talker. In the next twenty minutes, I learned more about her personal history as a coffee drinker than I would ever need to know. By the time we were sitting at one of those little Starbucks tables, she had somehow done a segue into conversation that ranged from her social studies teacher to her brother's lousy table manners to how she got sparkle on her nails.

I listened attentively. I looked into her eyes. I looked down at her nails. I did not look at her breasts, even after she spilled some coffee on one of them, nor did I offer to wipe the spilled coffee off, though I was sorely tempted. *Keep your mind on the goal,* I told myself. *Keep your eyes up; lay on the praise.*

After an hour, I think I had complimented her eyes (many times), her smile (many times), her teeth (a couple), her laugh (once), her voice (several), her wit (once), her insight (once) and her math skills (a cost comparison of lattes versus espressos— once). I didn't even have time to use my joke (memorized) and my obscure coffee facts (taken from the Internet) in case of any awkward silences. There were no silences, awkward or otherwise. So I figured it was time.

"Have you seen that new Jim Carrey movie at the Capitol? It's supposed to be pretty funny." I tried to sound cool and offhand, as if this were just idle conversation.

"No, not yet," she said. "I'd like to, though."

"How about tomorrow night? Are you busy?"

"Well, I'm supposed to babysit. But how about next Saturday?"

"That would be great," I said. "I'll check the times and give you a call. Oh yeah, I need your number."

"Oh, sure," she said. She grabbed a brown Starbucks napkin and wrote out her phone number in big block printing. Then she stuffed it in my pants pocket so I couldn't lose it.

When we left Starbucks, I wasn't sure whether I should walk her home or not. She made the answer pretty clear by grabbing my hand. It wasn't long before we got to her house and she had to go in.

"Thanks for walking me," she said in about the sweetest voice I'd ever heard.

"No problem," I blurted out. I think ninety minutes of attentive niceness was about my limit.

"And just one thing, Alan," she said. "You've got a little bit of cappuccino on your upper lip."

"Up here?" I said, reaching up with my hand.

"No," she replied, "bend over and I'll get it."

So I did, and suddenly I felt her lips on mine, and then her tongue seemed to swipe over my upper lip.

"There," she said while I tried to breathe again. "That got it. See you Saturday."

I stood there, unable to speak. I had been kissed. I hadn't asked for a kiss, or expected a kiss or even deserved a kiss, but I got one. I felt like shouting, "HEY, I JUST GOT MY VERY FIRST REAL KISS!" But instead I stood there, dumbfounded.

"Call me," she said.

"I will," I sighed. "I will." And then she was gone, dancing up the steps to her front door.

# 7

# More Instructions

SOMEHOW I MADE it to my house. For once in my life, I was unaware of my clunky feet and my awkward body. I floated. My mind was stuck on that wonderful moment when her lips touched mine. It was spectacular.

I must still have been beaming from Mel's kiss when I sat down at the dinner table. My mother gave me a peculiar look.

"You're looking very cheerful, Alan," she said.

"Yeah, well, I'm feeling cheerful," I told her. "I've got a date for next Saturday."

"A date?" she said. "That's wonderful," she cooed. This must be one of those great moments in parenting, the son gets his very first date. "Who's the lucky girl?"

"Melissa Halvorsen," I said.

"I think I know her dad," my father piped up. "Big guy. Used to be a wrestler or something."

"I'm not dating her dad, Dad."

"Well, do have a good time," my mother said. "And be respectful. Girls always like that. Respect and good manners are so important."

"So you got tongue!" Jeremy shouted. "I can't believe it. You take the chick out for coffee and you got tongue."

"Just a little tongue," I told him.

"Al, you are a mover, I mean a *mover*. All this time, I figured you were just watching the Weather Channel, but you must have been working on your technique. The way you're going, she'll probably jump your bones right in the movie."

"I don't know."

"Well, I do," Jeremy said. "The important thing is to move fast. No more nice-guy stuff—move as fast as you can and get as much as you can, if you know what I mean."

I wasn't sure what Jeremy meant, but I pretended I had some idea. I gave him a conspiratorial wink, as if my sex life were about to reach levels not even reported in *Maxim* magazine.

I emailed Maggie about the upcoming date and she replied with a few encouraging words. But when I actually saw Maggie at school the next week, she gave me a weird look. It was almost as if she were studying my face. It made me feel awkward.

"She kissed you, didn't she."

"How can you tell?"

"You've got that look—that mixture of amazement and lust," she replied, shaking her head. "I should have remembered that Mel's not all that innocent. She's had a boyfriend. From the rumours after they split up, they went a long way."

"Really?" My ears pricked up.

"But don't get your hopes too high, Al. Just don't blow it on the first date. Who knows, a girl who'll give you a kiss even before the first date might just be the one to get you to the Ultimate Goal."

I said nothing, but my mind was running rampant.

"Anyhow, I've written out a second set of instructions. Study these and don't screw up."

**Project: Alan**
Instruction set 2

Review the previous instruction set. Memorize it. Take this test:
1.  My eyes should be focussed on (a) her eyes, (b) her boobs, (c) the floor.
2.  The biggest interest that Mel has is (a) herself, (b) you, (c) school.

3.  If you're stuck, you can always talk about (a) Mel's eyes, (b) computers, (c) Mr. Greer.

If you chose answer (a) in each case, you're ready to proceed. If you chose answer (b), you're hopeless and should go into a monastery or buy a trenchcoat and rent DVDs. Answer (c) merely shows confusion; go back and study the previous memo.

I'm assuming you passed the test. I've got faith in you, Al. You can do this.

**First-date basics:**
1.  Your goal for now is a second date. Focus on the second date.
2.  Be patient. Patience is one of the seven virtues (we'll ignore the others for a while). Do not push the Ultimate Goal.
3.  Do not grope, manhandle or squeeze any body parts, even if offered the opportunity to do so. See point 2, on patience, above.
4.  Above all, do not remove clothing or place your hand beneath said clothing: this is a serious first-date no-no. That's what second dates are all about.
5.  Be attentive, charming, funny and polite. (Review previous notes.)
6.  Don't rush a conclusion to the date if things are going well. (There's that patience thing again.)

**What to talk about:**
As you've already discovered, Mel likes to do all the talking. Relax and listen. Everybody likes a good listener, even me.

**Things not to say:**
1.  Oops, my hand slipped.
2.  I thought *you* were paying for the ticket.
3.  Do you always put on lipstick a little crooked?
4.  Whatever is making me itch, I don't think it's contagious.
5.  Have you ever thought about trying Dr. Phil's new diet?

**Some notes on kissing:**

I realize that you've already gotten one kiss, but that's only a beginning. Since most guys haven't got a clue about kissing, let me give you a few pointers:

1. A kiss is a culmination of feeling, it isn't a starter. Thus it's better to wait for the right moment than to thrust out your lips too soon.

2. Your breath and/or gleaming smile is not nearly as important as Clorets would have you believe. Nonetheless, garlic must be a joint venture and a bit of gum never interfered with a kiss.

3. A good kiss starts with dry, closed lips, not with a gaping wet mouth.

4. Tilt your head to the right to avoid nose collisions.

5. After a soft, dry kiss, run your tongue along her upper lip. (There's a lot of sensitive skin there and virtually none inside her mouth.)

6. If, and only if, she opens her mouth, send your tongue in a little deeper.

7. Do not perform a tongue tonsillectomy. It is the touching of tongues that is erotic. Be soft, gentle and playful.

8. Leave her wanting more. Do not continue kissing until your lips are sore or there's saliva running down your chins. As Corbusier said, Less is more.

Who is Corbusier, I wondered, and how did he learn so much about women? Still, the advice seemed pretty good to me. I practised kissing the back of my right hand to see if I could get the technique down: dry, soft and sexy. I must admit that my right hand thought I had it down just right, but it tends to be pretty easy on such matters.

*I was ready,* I told myself.

*You're ready,* my right hand agreed.

# 8

# An Awkward Moment or Two

I'm glad our town is walkable. One of the miserable things about being just seventeen is that a full driver's licence kills your family's car insurance, and a learner's permit isn't good enough to drive by yourself. I know there are guys who still let their parents play chauffeur, but that makes me feel like I'm twelve. Fortunately, our town isn't that large. There might be a dozen streets between the harbour and the college up the hill, maybe two dozen stretching along the length of Main Street. Mel lived only five blocks from my house, and the movieplex was close to her place. *Walking is cool,* I told myself as I walked in the early-April damp. Besides, walking gives you an excuse to hold hands, and holding hands gives an excuse for a kiss, and a kiss . . .

*Whoa,* I told myself. *Focus on the first date. Be patient. Stick to the instructions.*

I got to Melissa's house and pushed the doorbell. This turned on some chimes that played "We Are the Champions" in some electronic bell-like tones. A second later and the door was opened by Mel's brother, a guy who had the unfortunate name of Valentine. Of course he was as large as a Buffalo Bills linebacker.

"The jerk is here!" he shouted.

I smiled. It never pays to irritate the brother of your date, especially when he could easily break you in two.

"Val, shut up!" came Mel's voice from somewhere upstairs. "Tell him I'll be down in a second."

"Motormouth says she's coming," he told me. "Guess you can go sit someplace."

With that wonderful welcome, the linebacker disappeared and left me standing in the hall. *Oh well,* I said to myself, *at least she doesn't have a large slobbery dog.* I've had a thing about large dogs ever since a traumatic face-licking when I was three, or so my mother says. Miserable older brothers are nothing compared to large dogs.

I thought about sitting in the living room, where a hockey game was filling a giant television, but decided it would be better to stand. I balanced on my feet and wondered if I should have brought flowers. On the TV dating shows, guys always bring flowers. Why hadn't I thought of flowers? Then again, if I had brought flowers, I can just imagine the response of Mel's brother. So I waited, flower-less and awkward.

In a couple of minutes, Melissa came flouncing down the stairs. She looked incredible, dressed in tight-everything, her little tank top revealing a very nice navel. But I didn't stare; I didn't even look for more than a second. Really, I didn't.

"You are so gorgeous!" I said, and I meant it.

The linebacker appeared at that point and let out a long belch. "Give me a break!" he groaned. "Mel, you look like a slut."

"Shut up, reject," she replied.

"Me, a reject? You're the reject. And you look like a slut."

"And you look like an ape. So stuff it."

"Stuff yourself."

"C'mon, Al, let's get out of here."

A second later we were outside, safely removed from the opinionated linebacker.

"Your brother is, uh"—I searched for a word—"outspoken."

"My brother is a total jerk," she said straightforwardly. "But thanks for not noticing."

"And you really do look great," I said, focussing on her eyes.

"You are so sweet," she said, and she gave me a quick kiss on the cheek and took my hand.

Mel had a lot more to say about her brother, some of which I even listened to. But mostly I was thinking about that very nice quick kiss and the easy way we held hands. This whole dating thing wasn't nearly as hard as people said it would be—you just had to relax and let it happen.

We got in line to buy the movie tickets, and then I went over to the refreshment counter to pick up the Double Double Special—basically a couple of Cokes and a wastebasket full of tasteless popcorn. I was still feeling pretty good about all this. My first date, and everything was going just fine—swimmingly, as Jeremy would say on one of his British days.

The two of us headed into the theatre and settled into our seats. It was one of those theatres where the seats tilt back a little, so in no time we were leaning back, side by side, trying to make a dent in the popcorn.

Up on the screen were those slides that pretend to be a movie quiz but are really ads for upcoming attractions. You know the kind: "What exciting new comedy is Hugh Grant appearing in next month?" Mel was quick coming up with the answers, aided by her regular viewing of Star TV.

At one point, she dribbled some popcorn on her top, which then tumbled down to her tummy and ended up right in the indentation of her navel.

"Oops."

I had to notice. I also had to laugh. Then I grabbed the misplaced piece of popcorn and quickly popped it into my mouth.

"You're so romantic," she said, and then gave me a quick buttery kiss. Okay, so it was actually a golden-topping kiss, but I liked it just as much. I replied with another kiss, this one a little more substantial. Then I remembered Maggie's list, so pulled back and gave a lick along her upper lip.

She pulled back and shivered. "And you're so sexy," she added.

I smiled to myself. I doubt that I'm either romantic or sexy, but I do know how to follow instructions.

The lights finally went down and the movie started. We watched the show for a while, and then Mel kind of nestled her head on my shoulder. So I did the natural thing and put my arm around her shoulder, and that left my hand kind of dangling there. I thought for a second about a quick grope, but then remembered my instructions and put my hand on her upper arm. Then I got really smart and began running my finger up and down the skin of her arm.

I wish there was some easy way of knowing when girls start getting turned on. With guys, it's pretty obvious unless you're wearing really tight jockey shorts. But with girls, you have to try to interpret their breathing, their sighs and just how they position their heads. If only there were a manual on all this, I could tell for sure that Mel was getting excited, but at that moment I only had a hunch to work on. My hunch was, yeah, Mel was getting turned on.

So it was time for some serious kissing. I was up to point seven in the instructions—avoid giving a tongue tonsillectomy. Then again, Mel was doing a pretty effective job with her tongue, too. Our tongues and lips were so busy that we missed most of the movie, but that was fine with me.

When the credits rolled at the end of the flick, we had to disentangle ourselves. This was no mean feat, because my arm seemed permanently crimped around her shoulders and my hand was entwined in her hair. Then there was the standing-up problem because, as I explained, with guys it's pretty obvious when we get excited.

Still, we made it to the aisle, and then out of our theatre to the lobby. I had one arm around Mel's waist and she had one arm around mine. At that moment, I had a stroke of genius.

Most people were getting on an escalator leading up to the main floor, but off to one side was an elevator—probably for the handicapped and the elderly. *But what about an elevator for the horny,* I said to myself.

"Let's take the elevator," I said.

"Why?" she asked.

"It'll be more private," I told her. And that got a little giggle.

So while the rest of the patrons made a file to go up the escalator, Mel and I snuck off to the elevator and waited for the doors to open. When they did, we slipped inside, and I pressed the close-door button.

"Aren't you going to press for the main floor?" Mel asked.

"You in a hurry?" I replied, pulling her into my arms.

It was a chance for some serious, body-to-body kissing. It was time for hands to run all over each other.

I suppose I should have remembered Maggie's rules—especially number three, the one about groping—but groping is such a wonderful thing, and I wasn't doing all the groping myself. I must say that Mel's hands were busy all over me. In fact, the two of us were so busy with the mutual kissing and groping that neither of us felt the elevator begin to move.

And then I forgot rule four, the one about hands and clothing. Above all, do not remove clothing or place your hand beneath said clothing. That's what Maggie had written.

But with all that groping going on, my hands seemed to have a mind of their own. One hand sneaked under Mel's tank top and began groping there. Another hand made its way down inside the back of her jeans. If I'd had a third hand, I suspect that one would have gotten me in trouble too.

"Alan," Mel said, pulling away from me. "Slow down."

And I could have slowed down, really. I could have pulled both hands away and followed instructions. But I kept hearing Jeremy's voice saying *Go for it*. There was a debate going on in my mind, like those devil-vs.-angel debates you see in cartoons, except in my case it was Maggie vs. Jeremy. Meanwhile, my hands were making their own decisions.

Mel was not responding well. "Alan, cut it—"

She didn't have time to finish. The elevator door opened on the main floor. Suddenly we were in full view of the crowd leaving the show. And who should be waiting near the elevator but Allison Mackenzie and her friend Rachel, the two biggest gossips in the school.

We were caught—red handed, in my case; red faced in Mel's.

"Eww," Allison commented when she saw the two of us, entwined.

"I always heard that Mel was easy," Rachel said.

Their eyes—and the eyes of a dozen other people—stared at us. I was frozen, like a deer caught in the headlights of a car.

"Alan, let go," Mel ordered.

And I tried. I managed to get the hand out of her tank top without too much trouble, but the hand that had slithered down her jeans got stuck. Somehow my watch got caught in her belt, or something like that, but my hand just wouldn't get out.

"Look, he's out of control," Allison said in that waspish way she has.

"Al's one horny guy," Rachel added.

And then the laughter began. Not just the two of them, but the whole crowd of people waiting in the lobby.

"Alan, I'm warning you," Mel told me.

"I'm trying . . .," I said.

"I told you to stop," she said.

"I'm trying," I repeated.

This entire exchange, and the laughter, might have lasted all of three seconds—certainly no more than four. But each of those seconds felt like an eternity; each of those seconds has been replayed in my brain a thousand times; each of those seconds will live in infamy.

It was Mel who finally stopped all the embarrassment. She took a deep breath and then, very quickly, brought up her knee. It connected with amazing force right between my legs, right *there*.

"Oh . . .," I groaned, adding a swear word for emphasis. I saw little flashing lights in front of my eyes, but the pain down below was glowing a dull red. I had trouble breathing, trouble seeing and trouble talking.

"You pig!" Mel shouted, somehow freeing herself from my errant hand.

There was a round of applause from the group watching all this. Then Mel went stomping off self-righteously while I stood helplessly in the elevator.

At that moment, it seemed as if certain parts of my body would never function again, not ever. And I'm not just talking about my very embarrassed face.

# 9

# In Disgrace With Fortune and Men's Eyes

"YOU BLEW IT," Maggie told me at school on Monday. We were sitting in the lunch room. She had offered me that three-word summary the minute she sat down in the empty chair across from me.

"How'd you know?" I asked. My mom had given me celery sticks, and I hate celery sticks, but that was the least of my problems.

"Everybody knows, Al. Everybody. Mel didn't get that 'Motormouth' nickname for nothing."

"She told . . . everybody?" I gulped.

"Just her friends. And then her friends told their friends. Then Hannah got the news and the rumour mill really got spinning. And that was Sunday. By third period today everyone in school heard that you were an orangutan on the date, and that you tried to take her clothes off in the elevator."

"Really?"

"Mel exaggerates a little," Maggie said. "I think she's using the phrase 'sexual assault' or something like that." Maggie was acting like this was quite normal, as if the trashing of my reputation were no more unusual than an upcoming math test. "When I got the story, you attacked her in the elevator but she had the presence of mind to get the elevator moving and then knee you because you were so out of control."

"Out of control?" I screamed.

People in the cafeteria craned their necks to look. I turned red in the face. They were all looking at me, looking at a guy out of control.

"I'm just telling you the story I got," Maggie said in a low voice. "Nobody really believes all that. After the tales Mel told about her last boyfriend, you got off pretty easy. She could have gone to the police and charged you."

I was sweating heavily at this point. Maggie was right, of course. The whole thing could have been worse, much worse.

"So what really happened?" she asked.

"I . . . uh . . . I broke rule two, the one about patience."

"And probably rules three and four about groping," Maggie suggested.

"Yeah, those too," I admitted. My voice was choked up and I wanted to die. I wanted to disappear. I wanted to take a big jump like those guys in *The Matrix* and get myself out of school, away from everything. "So what do I do now?"

"Start over," Maggie said, her voice doing a tonal shrug. "You fell flat on your face, so all you can is get up, survey the damage and begin again. Wait a week or so for the rumours to die down and then we'll find some other girl."

"Like who?"

"Don't know yet," she said. "I've got to ask around and find out if anybody is into out-of-control guys." She shook her head, looking at me almost with pity. "Okay, Al, it was just a joke. Just leave the problem with me and I'll get back to you."

I felt a large shape looming behind me. Maggie looked up.

"You ready to go?" came a voice from over my shoulder.

I turned and saw none other than Braden Boyce standing behind me. Even from this angle, his face was perfectly shaped, like that of a Greek statue. The bonus, of course, is that Braden wasn't Greek. He came from one of the old-money families in town, the kind of family where Grandpa's picture is up at the country club for winning the tournament of '22 and Dad's picture is up at the yacht club as commodore of the summer regatta, 1998. Not that I have ever been to the country club or the yacht club, but you get the idea.

"Ready in a second," Maggie replied. "I'll meet you down at the car."

That seemed enough to satisfy Braden. His shadow disappeared and that left just Maggie and me.

"So those rumours are true," I mumbled.

"Which rumours?"

"That you've hooked up with Braden."

Maggie thought for a second. "Hook up is too strong a verb," she said. "I kind of like him and he probably figures, if he does the right moves, that maybe he'll get laid."

I wasn't sure what to say, but I guess my face asked the obvious question.

"But I doubt it," Maggie added, before getting up to follow her boyfriend to the parking lot.

I had a hunch that Maggie would eventually give in to him. Guys like Braden Boyce are always getting laid. All they have to do is blink their perfect blue eyes, flash their perfect white smiles, and the girls are all over them. In Braden's case, all he had to do was drive up in that BMW roadster and he has girls fighting to get in the back seat—and there's no back seat!

I sucked on a celery stick. Here I was, dateless, chickless, despised, rejected, disgraced. My life had taken a sudden tumble. It's like that little-kids' game, Snakes and Ladders. You just think you're about to finish when, zam, you land on the wrong square and end up back at the beginning.

I was feeling truly and deeply sorry for myself at that point, but I knew that wouldn't do any good. I had to project confidence. I had to show everybody that Mel's accusations were false; that a guy as cool and self-confident as me couldn't possibly have done what she said. I had to get up and stand like a man who was proud of himself, a man innocent of all charges.

Besides, I said to myself, things couldn't get worse.

I kept believing that all the way to my locker. I kept my head high, my eyes straight, a firm smile on my face. I could tough this out. I could start over and rebuild. I could—

"There he is!"

"Grab him!"

In less than a second, I was pushed from the hallway into the guy's washroom. The push was so fast and so effortless that I should have known a football player was at the muscled end of it.

"You pervert!" Val spat in my face. "I heard what you tried to do to my sister."

"I didn't."

"Don't try to BS me," he went on. Val Halvorsen had one beefy hand at my neck and another clenched into a fist. One of his buddies held my left wrist in a Vulcan death grip; another had my right arm in some kind of wrestling hold.

"I didn't. I never." I am not articulate at the best of times. In a situation like this, I was reduced to the vocabulary of a two-year-old.

"You're gonna pay for this, Macklin," Val went on. "You're gonna wish you were never born."

I am actually reducing his speech somewhat, dropping out the swear words that he used as punctuation. With each swear word, he seemed to be spitting in my face.

"This is just for starters," Val said, and sent his clenched fist into my gut.

I would have doubled over in pain, but the other two guys literally held me up against the wall.

"And this—"

Val's words were cut off when the door opened. Over his shoulder I could see Mr. Greer, probably on smoker patrol. I had never, in my life, been so glad to see a teacher.

"Ah, Mr. Greer," I managed to say.

"Are you gentlemen having a discussion?" Mr. Greer asked.

"Uh, no," Val said, his voice suddenly sweetness and light. "We were talking about, uh, imperfect fractions. We were just giving Al a little study session because, like, he's got a few problems."

That, I realized, was an understatement.

## 10

# If at First . . .

IF AT FIRST YOU don't succeed, try, try again. What kind of idiot came up with an idea like that? If at first you don't succeed, give up and go try something else. For the next few days, I considered life in a monastery. After a little Internet research, I figured I could be a very effective Benedictine monk. They have a simple life: no women, no talking, no making a fool of yourself. Besides, they make a very fine brandy that probably gets tested in the monastery before it's shipped out to the rest of the world.

I was being treated like a leper at school, a *pariah* to use Jeremy's word. I'm not sure that being a pariah is worse than being a leper, but it certainly sounds worse. On top of all that, I had to keep a wary eye out for Val Halvorsen and his football buddies. I suspect they had some cruel and unusual punishment in mind for me, something like disassembling my body parts, or maybe worse.

"You need a bodyguard," Jeremy told me. "Somebody like Moose Mulkiwich."

Moose Mulkiwich had been the biggest kid in our class ever since kindergarten. By grade four he was taller than the teacher, by grade eight he had to duck to fit through the classroom door. Unfortunately, he is also the most gentle person I've ever met and he's probably never been in a fight.

"Don't think so," I replied. "He's not mean enough."

"How about Ratsy Malone? He's already been arrested a couple of times. He's small and wiry, but probably a little dangerous."

"Yeah, he used to steal milk money from me five years ago." I sighed. "But I'm not sure I want to give him the business."

"So I guess you take your chances," Jeremy told me.

In truth, the physical danger didn't bother me as much as the general embarrassment—that pariah thing. Even friends like Scrooge were pretending they didn't really know me, or acting like I'd had some kind of seizure that night at the movies.

Rubbing the whole thing in were my parents. "Whatever happened to that Halvorsen girl you were dating?" my dad asked.

"We only had one date," I mumbled. I was midway through a bit of mashed potatoes. My father is a master of asking questions at that midway point, when any answer means spitting out your food or swallowing it in a lump.

"Didn't work out?" he went on.

"You could say that," I replied. I washed down the potatoes with milk.

"You did respect her, didn't you? That's so important," he told me.

"Of course," I lied, "of course."

*What is respect?* I asked myself. It's like a *Jeopardy* question: a six-letter word with two *e*'s, starting with *r* and ending in *t*. That's all. The dictionary says it means you have "to show deferential regard" to someone. Why should I show deferential regard to a girl who was literally climbing all over me in the movie but then gets embarrassed when her friends catch her in an awkward clinch in the elevator? I mean, if I were Brad Pitt, she would have been proud to have my hand stuck in her . . . Okay, forget that. It was a bad moment in my life; one of those shame-filled moments that will come back to haunt me for the next thirty years or so. It could have been worse. That's what I have to keep telling myself—it could have been worse.

On Thursday, Maggie found me while I was eating my lunch. She seemed unusually cheerful, or perhaps it was just in contrast to how I felt.

"I've got good news and bad news," she began. "I assume you want the bad news first, courageous guy that you are."

"Of course," I replied, smiling faintly. "It's not enough that my friends have abandoned me and everybody else thinks I'm a pariah. I really do need more bad news."

She ignored my sarcasm.

"Okay, it's time for your first bill," she said. "Let me know if this is in order."

### Maggie McPherson Consulting
Statement of Account for March


Project: Alan

| | |
|---|---|
| Initial consultation | $5.00 |
| Instruction set #1 | 21.00 |
| First date, Mel Halvorsen | 25.00 |
| Counselling | 10.00 |
| Second date, MH | 5.00 |
| Instruction set #2 | 26.00 |
| Website setup | 10.00 |
| | |
| Total for March | $102.00 |
| Less retainer | 50.00 |
| | |
| Installment now due | $52.00 |

Your patronage and prompt payment is always appreciated.

"You realize that this adds insult to injury," I told her.

"A very effective cliché, Alan, but you did sign a contract and I delivered on my end of the deal. Instructions—done; two dates—complete. It's really not my fault if you forget my instructions and lose control of yourself," she said. "Any other issues?"

"What's this thing about a website setup? What website?"

Maggie positively beamed at me. She has unusually large cheeks when she smiles, cheeks accentuated by her freckles so that she sometimes resembled a red-headed squirrel.

"It's part of the good news," she told me. "If the bill is in order and the cash is forthcoming, I'll give you the rest of the good news."

I did a mental calculation of the cash in my bank account: $642 less the $50 I'd already given her left me with roughly $590, so I could afford the money. And I really did owe it to her, given the contract and all.

"You take Visa?" I asked.

"Sorry, cash or cheque," she replied.

"I was kidding. I'll bring you the cash tomorrow. Now what's the rest of the good news?"

"I found a girl who'll go out with you," she said brightly.

"Under a rock?" I asked.

"No, at St. Agnes. Hidden away in her posh private school, she hasn't heard a thing about the Mel Halvorsen fiasco. In fact, all she knows about you is what she's heard from me, delivered in suitably glowing terms. A little exaggeration is all part of the service, Al."

"She's not an ugger, is she?" I asked.

"No, the girl I have in mind is really quite beautiful if you like that vapid Nordic blonde look. In fact, she's so beautiful that most guys are afraid to ask her out. She's ripe for a boyfriend, Al, and that could be you."

"What's her name?"

"I'll give you her name and more details when I get my second installment. It's not that I don't trust you, Al, but this is a business transaction. And I should remind you, when we go forward you're into a new billing period, of course, with the usual charges."

"Yeah, yeah, I get the picture," I said. "But you still haven't explained the website."

"It was part of building you up," Maggie said. "I was telling the girl in question what a great guy you are, and she asked the obvious question of why you didn't have a girlfriend. I couldn't tell her about the Mel problem, so I made up something about an old girlfriend who didn't work out. A bit like Rosaline in *Hamlet*."

"Yeah, sure." I really have to read that play some day.

"But then I thought, what if she Googles you?"

"Googles me?"

"Yeah, what if she put your name into Google to see what comes up. Mel already has a website up called Alanthejerk.com but it doesn't have your last name. So I set up a site called AlanCome Back.com. It talks about how much a girl named Rosaline misses you, and how wonderful you are, and how she wants you back."

"Very creative," I said.

"I thought so. So AlanComeBack.com is what this girl will get if she Googles you."

I sighed. "Maggie, sometimes I think you're a genius."

She smiled in triumph. "Sometimes I do, too."

## 11

# Practice Makes Perfect

I RATHER LIKED the AlanComeBack.com site. Maggie had put together a number of low-res photos that showed somebody, presumably me, out hiking or dining or laughing with a girl named Rosaline. Then there were some fond memories of our "time together" and a plea for me to "give it another chance." I found the whole site so touching that I really would have given Rosaline another chance, if only she had actually existed.

Of course, I also had to check out Alanthejerk.com. It had only one photograph, of Mel delivering the finger to (presumably) me, and an awful collection of nasty comments about yours truly. Some were complete with descriptive language unsuitable for children, others had threats along the lines of "If I ever see you again, your . . . will be stuck so far up your . . . that you'll never . . . again," with some colourful words in place of the ellipses.

I wasn't sure whether to be proud or embarrassed about my sudden prominence on the Internet. Nonetheless, I was glad that AlanComeBack.com was on the first Google page that came up if you typed in my name.

So the next day, I brought Maggie the cash for her fee and received, in return, a photo, a phone number and an email address for a girl named Taylor Hoskin. It was the photo that made my jaw drop—Taylor Hoskin really was a Nordic beauty. She had fine blonde hair, pale eyebrows, flawless skin, gorgeous blue eyes, and a general resemblance to Gwyneth Paltrow.

"Why do guys go so ga-ga over a decent-looking blonde?" Maggie snapped back. "You don't even know what kind of person she is."

That was true, so I apologized for guys everywhere who begin drooling over the mere picture of a beautiful girl. It is a defect in the male personality, I think, that we are so swayed by good looks. For all I knew, Taylor Hoskin could be an axe murderer; she could be a terrible tease; she could be a snob to her girlfriends; she could be dumb as a doorknob. Nonetheless, I found my heart beating faster just holding her picture in my hand.

By Maggie's report, Taylor was not a tease, a snob or a doorknob. She was a bright, pretty girl who just happened to play on Maggie's soccer team. Taylor was apparently an excellent forward with a mean kick—something that made me a little wary after my last date.

Taylor's father was a surgeon in town and the family lived up on Mayfair Drive, in a modern mansion built to resemble an ancient Greek temple. For whatever reason, Taylor Hoskin was dateless— and thus ripe for me.

Maggie suggested I begin by emailing her. "Be funny," she told me, "and keep them short. In fact, you better copy me in on each one."

"Maybe you should write them," I suggested.

She did a mental calculation. "That would be ten bucks a message, Al. Unless you have money to burn, I suggest you give up on the *Cyrano de Bergerac* approach."

Since I had no idea what a *Cyrano de Bergerac* approach might be, I decided to do the emails myself. I can write a rather amusing email, I'm told, and these are frequently appreciated by my grandmother and Aunt Betty, the usual recipients, who often comment on my excellent spelling.

"Be flirtatious but not pushy," Maggie told me.

"Exactly what I had in mind," I said.

The prospect of a date with Taylor Hoskin—actually, the prospect of a date with *anyone*—lifted my spirits considerably. I began smiling a bit in class. I even talked to my parents over dinner. And I felt relaxed enough to let down my guard against Val Halvorsen and the goons who wanted to stick my . . . so far up my . . . that I'd never . . . again.

My improved spirits were finally noticed by Jeremy. He commented that no one in my position should be as cheerful as I seemed to be.

So I told him the truth. "Maggie is hooking me up with a girl from St. Agnes," I said, trying hard not to brag too much.

"No way," he spluttered.

"Her father is, how shall I say this, an important person in the medical community and the girl herself, well, somewhat resembles Gwyneth Paltrow."

Jeremy gave me a look that mingled disbelief and scorn. "And she's going to go out with you?"

I decided that Jeremy was asking a rhetorical question that did not really deserve an answer. I admit, I had thought about the question he raised—how would a smart, rich, beautiful girl respond when she actually met me, a rather ordinary, poor and homely guy? On the other hand, there are many fairy tales about princesses falling in love with frogs, so perhaps anything is possible.

The email correspondence went quite well. It was actually a three-way chain: I'd send a draft to Maggie; she'd make corrections and return it to me; I'd send the email to Taylor; then I'd forward the reply to Maggie.

People say that the Internet has killed the art of letter writing, and that may be, but there isn't much connection between a short, highly abbreviated email and the great love letters of the past. Here's how it began.

> From: mackman@ibid.net
> To: tmhoskin@fonzie.com
> Hey, my name is Alan and I used to play soccer with ur friend Maggie McPherson, at least until the coach discovered I had been born with 2 left feet. :-) Anyhow, life has moved on and I've grown up to be tall, dark, handsome and terrifically witty. Or whatever. Maggie thinks we might be perfect for each other, and she's frequently right about a lot of things. So long as you

don't ask me to play soccer (I hear ur wicked) we might
have a lot in common.

From: tmhoskin@fonzie.com
To: mackman@ibid.net
Hey, Alan. Maggie says you're cute and funny and you
were always a lousy soccer player, regardless of your
feet. One thing I know for sure, you've got to be more
attractive than anybody here at St. Agnes! :-) ;-)

The correspondence continued in a similar vein for almost two
weeks. I don't think the emails got any more profound or interesting, but they did lead to the phone call that got me a dinner date. I
decided that a girl of this quality—a surgeon's daughter, after all—
deserved the best.

"You're planning a snow job" is what Jeremy said.

"A what job?" I replied.

"A snow job," he said. "That's when you try to seduce the chick
with your money, class and *savoir faire*. She's so snowed by the big
dinner out that she kind of throws herself at you."

"Sounds good to me."

"Where you taking her?" he asked.

"I was thinking about the Beef and Barrel."

Jeremy shot me a look. "You're going to take a girl who looks like
Gwyneth Paltrow to the Beef and Barrel? You're going to try to snow
a gorgeous chick—a doc's daughter—by buying her a T-bone? Alan,
let us get real!"

"Not the Beef and Barrel?"

"For a real snow job, you gotta go to Rayburn's," Jeremy declared.
"I once took a girl up there for dinner, did my little *savoir faire* thing,
and the next thing you know . . . well, I was a pretty happy camper."

There were so many strange metaphors in what Jeremy said that I
had a hard time making sense of it all. The implication was clear,
however. Dinner at Rayburn's improved a guy's chance of getting laid.

"Is it expensive?"

"Yeah. That's what makes for the snow job. You don't get lucky by taking a girl out to McDonald's, you gotta lay out some cash. Believe me, Al, I know what I'm talking about."

"Whooo," I sighed. "This whole project is getting expensive."

"It'll be worth it, Al. And I'm going to do you a favour. My dad has a buddy who's got a little limousine service. I bet I can score you a limo for, say, half price."

In retrospect, it seems a little over the top, but at the time I had this image of me—looking a bit like Brad Pitt—leading Taylor Hoskin—looking a lot like Gwyneth Paltrow—out of a stretch limousine and into some fabulous Hollywood restaurant. The simple fact that I don't at all resemble Brad Pitt, and that we don't live in Hollywood, still did not dispel the image. It seemed romantic, poetic, sensational . . . exactly what I needed to seduce the beautiful Taylor Hoskin.

"Rayburn's?" Maggie asked.

The two of us were at my house, after school, trying to get me ready for the dinner date. I had expected a set of instructions, but Maggie told me that I needed some more direct teaching. So now we were in the computer/TV/everything room on two rolling computer chairs.

"I hear it's quite elegant," I told her.

"And quite pricey," Maggie said. "If I knew you could afford to take somebody to Rayburn's, I would have raised my whole fee schedule."

I decided not to tell Maggie about the limousine. For one thing, I didn't know if Jeremy would be able to pull it off. Jeremy's record for follow-through is not really the best. For a second thing, I didn't think Maggie would approve. There was something about her attitude that day that seemed just a little strange.

"Okay, I've done a little analysis of the Mel fiasco, trying to get to the root of your problem," Maggie began.

"My problem?"

"Yes, your problem," Maggie replied, her voice serious. "It's not an uncommon problem for boys, probably a genetic defect passed on from generation to generation. My friends call it 'Roman hands and Russian fingers.'"

"Roman hands and . . . ah, roaming hands . . ."

"You're not alone in this, Alan, a lot of guys have this problem—you can't control your hands. Let's just recap the events. First, I give you perfectly good advice before the date. I believe I said explicitly, do not grope, manhandle or squeeze. And what did you do?"

"I groped."

"You also manhandled and probably squeezed."

This ought to have been funny, but Maggie was in a deadly serious mood. Her eyes were virtually breathing fire. This was an attractive look for Maggie. In fact, she had been looking quite good for the last week—something I attributed to Braden's influence. Her clothes were less baggy, her hair less frizzy, her eyes without glasses really quite large. If Maggie kept this up, she might actually turn out to be a bit of a babe.

"And so, Alan, I have decided that you require aversion therapy."

"What's that?"

"I was reading about it in *Psychology Today*. Basically, we have to train your nervous system to reject certain behaviours by associating them with pain or displeasure."

I looked at her. Maggie had the capacity to toss out something like that and actually expect that it would make sense to someone like me.

"So we're going to train you to control the 'Roman hands,'" Maggie said. "Now some of this may seem strange, but consider me your therapist as well as your adviser."

"Do I pay extra for this?"

"Just the usual ten dollars an hour," she said quickly, "but pay attention. For the next few minutes, I'm going to be Taylor Hoskin."

"You don't look like Taylor Hoskin," I said, grinning just a little.

"I'll ignore that," she snapped. "Let us assume that I *am* Taylor Hoskin or, for that matter, any girl. We are out on a date and have spent a nice evening together. Your hand accidentally brushes against my leg—so do it."

I brushed my hand against Maggie's leg. For the first time, I noticed that her skirt was really quite short.

She flinched. "Okay, and then your hand comes to rest naturally on my leg." She took my hand and put it on her knee.

"Actually, it would probably come to rest a little bit higher up," I said, adjusting my hand slightly.

"Okay," she said, so tense that she seemed to be holding her breath. "So now we talk for a while and what happens?"

So there we were, in two rolling computer chairs, my hand on Maggie's bare leg just above her knee, her eyes looking into my eyes. Half of me felt like laughing at how silly this was, and half of me was starting to get a little bit excited. After all, Maggie was a girl—a fairly attractive girl if you like that pushy redhead kind of woman—and my hand was nicely placed on a nicely shaped leg. So naturally I began to run my hand up her thigh, just a little, when—

*Whap!*

Maggie slapped me, right across the face.

"What?" I said, my cheek stinging. I raised my hand from her leg to bring some relief to my burning cheek.

"That's the aversion therapy," Maggie explained. "Your hand started roaming . . . uh, where it shouldn't, so the slap makes you associate that with physical pain. You do feel the pain, don't you?"

"Yeah, slap me in the face and I feel pain."

"Now we're going to try it again," Maggie said. "Put your hand back on my leg and keep it still. Do not—I repeat—do not let the hand climb up my leg!"

I was successful at this, really I was. I sat there for two, maybe three minutes with my hand resting quietly on Maggie's leg. Then I became aware of the warmth of her leg, its softness. I realized that Maggie was really far more attractive than I had thought before, that her lips were especially luscious and her eyes were very erotic. So my hand moved, just slightly—

*Whap!*

"You're getting better, Alan," Maggie said, looking down at her watch. "That was two and one half minutes."

I was holding on to my cheek, wincing in pain. Maggie herself was breathing hard, either from the situation or from the exertion of slugging me.

"Let's try it again," she said.

"But . . ."

"This is therapy, Alan. It's your only hope."

In all, we went through this routine five times. When I complained about the pain in my left cheek, she switched hands and slugged my right cheek. On the sixth attempt, I was able to keep my hand still and resist all temptation for a good twenty minutes.

"Excellent," Maggie declared. "You may be cured."

"Does this mean you're going to become a psychologist rather than a lawyer?"

"Absolutely not," she replied. "I'd far rather write you a memo than have to go through something like this again. So please, Alan, please don't mess up this time."

# 12

# My Limo, My Driver

JUST SO YOU don't think I'm a total idiot, let me explain that going to Rayburn's for dinner was not the first time I met Taylor Hoskin. After some days of emailing and a couple of phone calls, we decided to get together for coffee at the Starbucks near her school. I had already mastered the art of the coffee date with Mel: lots of praise, attentive listening, eyes on her eyes. This routine was much easier with Taylor because she was (a) beautiful, (b) intelligent and (c) had gorgeous light blue eyes. The only flaws I could detect in her appearance were minor: a slight gap between her two front teeth and a tendency to flip her blonde hair to produce a peculiar curl. Given the many flaws in my appearance and personality, I couldn't help but be amazed that a girl as perfect as Taylor would consent to sit and talk with me. But she did, and she seemed to find my praise, attention and romantic gaze—not to mention my wonderful sense of humour— more than a bit interesting. When I asked her out for a dinner date, she cheerfully agreed.

So when the day of my big date arrived, my expectations were high. Jeremy was instant messaging me that afternoon.

> BIG JERRY SAYS: Hey, Al, you're in luck. I got the limo
> for you.
> AL SAYS: Half price?
> BIG JERRY SAYS: 50 bucks. That's a deal. A couple
> cab rides would cost you almost that much.

Another fifty bucks. I had already taken a hundred dollars out of
the bank to pay for dinner and I probably owed Maggie another
fifty. If I didn't reach my Ultimate Goal pretty soon, I wouldn't have
enough cash to reach the summer.

> AL SAYS: 50 bucks isn't peanuts.
> BIG JERRY SAYS: When she sees the limo and you
> give her those flowers, she'll spread like butter.
> AL SAYS: What flowers?
> BIG JERRY SAYS: You gotta give her flowers, man.
> Don't you ever watch TV? You give her a big bouquet or
> one perfect red rose.

*Add another five bucks for a flower*, I said to myself.

> AL SAYS: Okay, I'll get the rose.
> BIG JERRY SAYS: You'll find a little present from me
> when the limo shows up. I think you'll like it.
> AL SAYS: Thanks in advance.
> BIG JERRY SAYS: Just don't do anything that I wouldn't
> do. lol
> AL SAYS: Fat chance!
> BIG JERRY SAYS: Don't sell yourself short. Play your
> cards right and this might be the night you get laid.

*I should be so lucky,* I thought, signing out.

A bit later, my father got home from work and saw me getting
dressed for the big event. I figured some kind of jacket would be a
good thing, since snooty restaurants will sometimes toss you out if
you don't have one. I even considered a tie, but that was going too
far. A blazer over khakis, that was the outfit, even if my dad's blazer
was a bit too small.

"Big date?" he asked me. My dad tries hard not to be pushy on
these things, but he can't resist asking.

"Yeah," I said. "A girl from St. Agnes."

"That's the all-girl school, isn't it?" he asked.

"Yeah. Really nice girl, too. Looks like Gwyneth Paltrow . . . and her dad is a brain surgeon." I knew that Dr. Hoskin was a surgeon, but I thought the "brain" part made him sound even more impressive.

"And she's going out with you?" My dad tried to control his amazement, but those were his words.

"A little miracle," I said. "I'm giving thanks to St. Agnes. And do you have any shoe polish?"

"Down in the basement. So . . . where are you two going, all dressed up like that?"

"Dinner," I replied. My mind was only half on this conversation. The other half was worried about something strange that was happening to my hair—something like spontaneous hat head.

"Not McDonald's," he said.

"No . . . the, uh, the Beef and Barrel." I'm not sure why I lied—maybe part of me knew that Rayburn's would be over the top. Maybe part of me knew that my parents had never, in their lives, gone to Rayburn's. My dad was a salesman for a small auto parts company and my mom did temp work. Big dinners at pricey restaurants weren't part of their budget or their lifestyle. So I lied, just so my dad wouldn't feel bad.

"Well, my little guy is growing up," my dad said. I believe there were tears forming in the corners of his eyes. "You have a great time tonight," he said, reaching into his pocket. "And maybe this will help."

He reached forward and stuck a ten-dollar bill in the blazer pocket.

"Hey, thanks, Dad."

He gave me a wink. "Just remember what's important with girls, Alan. Respect. Give her lots of respect."

I could have told my father that he'd been through the "respect" routine a few weeks ago, but decided to let it pass. This was one of those rare incidents of father–son bonding in our house, so it seemed a shame to spoil the moment.

Besides, after Maggie's therapy I was mastering self-control. Surely that was the largest part of respect.

I think I looked pretty good when I skipped out of the house: navy blazer, pressed shirt, clean khakis, some well-shined Dockers on my feet. I had a hundred dollars in my wallet and ten bucks in my blazer pocket, and one perfect red rose in my hand (cost $17.95, but never mind). I had asked the limo to come to Jeremy's house, just down the road, so my parents wouldn't see it. No sense rubbing it in, I thought.

I could see the limo from my front door, gleaming golden white under the setting sun, looking about as big as a yacht. The closer I got to the car, the bigger it became. When I got to it, the car looked like it had been stretched in a funhouse mirror—in fact, it was sagging slightly at the middle. Or maybe that's why I was able to get such a good deal.

The driver was waiting beside the limo, dressed in a smart uniform. He must have known I had arranged for it by my confident step as I walked up. He opened the back door for me, then stood at attention. "My name is Ahmed, sir, and I am your driver."

"Uh, great," I replied. I had never been called "sir" in my life.

The door slammed shut and I found myself in a massive compartment almost the size of my bedroom. If it had been any larger, Taylor and I could have set up a Ping-Pong table and played a game. Way up in front was a glass partition with curtains that separated the back section from the driver.

"Hello," I shouted.

Since there was no response, I figured that the partition was soundproof as well. So how was I supposed to talk to the driver? The answer came when Ahmed talked to me through a speaker.

"Where would we be going, sir?" he asked.

"321 Mayfair Drive," I shouted.

"You must press the talk button beside you, sir."

I looked at an array of buttons on the armrest and found one with a picture that looked vaguely like a microphone. I pressed it and repeated myself, trying to figure out the curious symbols on the other buttons at the same time. Which would open the sunroof? Which was really an ejection seat? My mind was already boggled.

"Yes, sir," Ahmed replied through the speaker. I felt the limo start to move, a bit like an ocean liner.

There may be a more wonderful experience than being chauffeured in a stretch limo, meeting a wonderful girl to head off for a fine dinner—for instance, I hope that sex is more wonderful—but since I don't know about sex, then all I can tell you is how wonderful I felt that evening. I stretched out in my stretch limo, played with buttons that opened the sunroof, turned on the radio, CD and television, and one that popped open a little bar.

Right there, in a little ice bucket, was a bottle of champagne.

Ahmed's voice came crackling through the speaker. "The champagne is a gift, sir, from Mr. Jeremy. He wishes you a very fine time, sir."

*What a friend!* I said to myself. *What a truly blessed life I lead— thank you, St. Agnes.* The patron saint of virgins was surely smiling on one of her own.

# 13

## One Large Slobbery Dog

WHEN WE REACHED TAYLOR'S house, Ahmed came racing around the limo to open the door for me. I got out and could imagine myself every bit a child of wealth and privilege. For a moment, I felt quite at home in front of the massive Greek columns, the sprawling front porch and the large green door. It was almost as if I did this kind of thing every day.

I walked onto the porch, raised the bronze ring of the door-knocker and tapped it three times. I tried to make it an authoritative tap. For my whole life, I told myself, I've been too tentative. From now on, I'm going to be authoritative. I will hold out my single, perfect rose and be authoritative, if not suave and debonair.

"Oh, hi," Taylor said when she opened the door. Then she saw the limo behind me, with Ahmed standing like a British soldier ready to salute the Queen. "What's that?"

"Our chariot," I said.

I thought that was quite poetic. Perhaps it was all going to my head even before the champagne. I held up the rose, but Taylor's eyes were fixed on the limo.

"Okay," she replied, her voice a bit wary. "So where are we going? I thought . . . maybe the Beef and Barrel?"

I tried not to laugh, really I did. Perhaps a little chuckle came out, but not a real laugh. Obviously the girl would soon be swept off her feet. "No, Rayburn's."

"Rayburn's!" she cried. "Why didn't you tell me? I've got to go change." She turned and looked into the house. "Mother!" she screamed, and then disappeared up the stairs.

For a few seconds, I was left standing alone in the front hall, still holding the rose. It was a very large hall, with a big central staircase, a crystal chandelier and several oil paintings of men who might be Dr. Hoskin or perhaps Dr. Hoskin's father.

I would have been quite comfortable waiting by myself, but I was soon joined by a huge dog—perhaps a cross between a German shepherd and a pit bull. Have I mentioned this problem I have with large dogs?

"Oh, hello," I said to the dog. I was trying desperately not to seem afraid. Large dogs always sense when you're afraid.

The dog snarled at me and bared his or her teeth.

"Ah, yes," I said, my voice climbing just a little higher. I tried to remember the best approach to dealing with a large, angry dog—did I stand still, hold out a hand, try to find a weapon? I remembered a unit on life in the Arctic—if attacked by a grizzly, hit it and run . . . or was that a black bear? And what did that have to do with a dog?

"Nice doggy," I said, pathetically. I wondered what would happen if I walloped the dog with the rose. Probably nothing.

The dog continued to growl and came closer. Soon it was within sniffing distance and I was petrified. The dog sniffed my foot, then my leg, and then stuck its nose right in my crotch.

I exhaled quickly. "Now, now, please don't bite," I told the dog. I spoke in the voice of a nursery school teacher trying to calm a class of out-of-control two-year-olds.

Fortunately, the dog did not bite; unfortunately, it licked. I suppose this was a friendly gesture, the dog licking my crotch, but I was still terrified. What's worse, my pants were getting soaked in dog saliva. In a minute it would look like . . . well, you know.

"Ginger, stop that," came a firm voice.

I looked up and saw a tall, blonde woman who must have been Taylor's mother.

"He's very friendly," the woman said.

"Ah, yes, I can see that," I replied. The dog was continuing to lick in the most embarrassing way.

"Ginger!" shouted the woman.

"Tie him up!" Taylor shouted from up the stairs. "Remember what happened . . ." She didn't complete the sentence.

The woman grabbed the dog by his collar and pulled him away from me. This gave me a chance to breathe a bit, and to look down at the damage. Khakis tend to darken when moistened with dog slobber, and the crotch of my pants was now soaking wet.

"I'm Taylor's mother," the woman announced, dragging the massive dog away, "and you must be Albert."

"Uh, Alan," I said.

"So nice to meet you," she said with a smile that revealed, like her daughter's smile, the same tiny gap between her two front teeth.

I think, at this point, we should have shaken hands, but Mrs. Hoskin was using both of hers to restrain the snarling Ginger. I thought of extending my hand, but I was afraid of what the dog might do if his mistress let go.

"Failed training school," she said, presumable referring to Ginger.

"So did my little brother," I replied. I tried to adjust the blazer so it covered the stain on my pants.

"Would I know your parents?" asked Mrs. Hoskin.

"Oh, I don't suppose so," I said. And then I got on a roll. "My father's at the university, sociology, I think. Or is it psychology? He keeps changing departments." I don't know what made me keep going. Perhaps I was terrified by the dog; perhaps I was driven by fear.

"And your mother?"

"She's a . . ." I looked around at the portraits and a word jumped out at me. "A judge. Not a high court or anything, I mean, not a Supreme Court judge but more like a middle-of-the-road judge. She, uh, judges things."

"I don't suppose they belong to—"

"Mother, you can stop the interrogation," Taylor told her as she came down the circular staircase. Then Taylor turned to me. "Now I'm ready."

I believe my jaw dropped. If my jaw did not drop, it should have dropped. The girl in front of me was the most magnificent female I had ever seen in real life, a fantasy made real. There is something about a little black dress, a bit of makeup and a pair of high heels that can transform a very pretty girl into every man's fantasy. In only a couple of minutes, while I was entertaining one snarling dog and one inquisitive mother, Taylor had transformed herself into a princess.

"You like the outfit?" she asked.

"I'm speechless," I said, with no exaggeration.

At this point, I was really at a loss. I was vaguely aware of a suspicious mother staring at me, a snarling dog ready to do damage to my body parts, and the wetness of my pants. However, I was mostly focussed on Taylor, her beauty, her perfume, her essence. I was transported.

"Please, take the flower. Its beauty is nothing compared to yours." I said that! I actually said that! I delivered a line of sheer poetry, a line of snow-job genius, and I did it with a straight face. I was instantly and hopelessly in love!

Taylor took the flower and handed it to her mother. "So let's go," she said.

We made it outside. For a second, I thought Ahmed might salute me as we came to the car. But he politely nodded and opened the door.

Taylor smiled and slid inside. I slid in beside her and quickly adjusted my blazer to cover the wet spot on my pants. Then Taylor and I both started to giggle.

"This is like being inside a Turkish bordello," she said.

I didn't admit my general lack of knowledge of Turkey or bordellos. I merely sighed. "You are so lovely."

"And you're over the top," she replied brightly. "What do you do for something like a prom?"

I thought for a second, and then it came to me: a brilliant moment of inspiration. "A helicopter!" I said. "I'll take you to your prom in a helicopter."

# 14

# A Little More Bubbly?

WITH THE TWO of us snuggling in the back of the limousine, I noisily uncorked the bottle of champagne and poured a glass for each of us. Taylor and I toasted life and stretch limos, while I mentally thanked Jeremy for this stroke of genius.

"Flowers, champagne, a limousine . . . Alan, I feel like I'm in a movie," Taylor said.

"For me, every minute with you is like a dream." I said that, too! I couldn't believe the lines that were coming out of my mouth.

She giggled; I giggled; we clinked glasses and giggled some more. She cuddled up beside me and I idly put my arm around her shoulders. Her little black dress had ridden up her legs, which were now pressed against mine.

*Oh, I could do well tonight,* I told myself.

But I stayed under control. Right there, right against me, were those fabulous legs. My hands were itching. My heart was beating. But I remembered Maggie's slap to the face and did nothing. *Be attentive, charming, funny and polite; be patient; do not grope or manhandle; do not push the Ultimate Goal; be patient, patient, patient.* I mentally reviewed all of Maggie's instructions. This time, I told myself, I would get it right.

We arrived at Rayburn's with a flourish and were taken to a romantic table in the corner. Sun was still streaming in the garden windows, and the light made Taylor's skin glow golden and perfect. I wanted to reach out and stroke her perfect cheek, but no, I kept my Roman hands under control.

"Good evening, Ms. Hoskin," said the waiter as he came up.

Obviously Taylor was no stranger here. "Could I offer you a cocktail, sir," he said to me.

"Well, uh, yes," I replied. I couldn't believe it—this waiter wasn't even going to ask for ID! Now I just had to think of a cocktail. What do people always ask for in movies? "A martini, please," I said.

"Shaken or stirred? Poured or straight up? Olive or lemon?"

"Uh, the usual," I said.

The waiter made a face as if I had just uttered a swear word in some language known to him and unknown to me. Then he leaned lower and spoke directly to me. "If I could just see some confirmation of your age, sir."

"Oh, sure," I replied, reaching into my wallet for the fake ID I had bought from Jeremy's cousin. The kid on the card looked only vaguely like me, but I figured the waiter was old enough that he couldn't see the difference without some reading glasses.

"Yes, thank you," he said, and then straightened up. "The usual, Ms. Hoskin?"

Taylor nodded and the waiter scurried off.

Taylor looked at me, a little embarrassed. "They know I'm too young to drink so I end up with these weird non-alcoholic things," she said. "But when you order the wine, if you get an extra glass . . ."

*Order the wine*, yes, indeed. I had never in my life ordered wine, but sooner or later I'd have to start. Tonight was the night. It was a night for new beginnings.

The drinks arrived along with the menus and the wine list. The menus were in oversized leather binders, something like the big books that teachers read in grade one, and the wine list was as long as the last novel I read. I opened both, stopping only to catch my breath when I saw the prices.

A bowl of soup cost my entire weekly allowance; a steak was the price of a small used car! Suddenly the $100 in my wallet seemed like a trifling amount.

"Why don't we skip appetizers?" I suggested.

"Oh, you have to try the beef carpaccio here," Taylor said. "Daddy says it's wonderful."

I looked at the menu—$18 for beef carpaccio. What is carpaccio, some kind of Italian parkade? Okay, if I have a cheap main course and Taylor pays half, this will work. But what if she doesn't pay half? Do restaurants still let you do dishes to pay off the bill?

I gulped.

"Have you selected the wine, sir?" asked the waiter.

"Wine, yes . . . the wine," I said. "Your list is so, uh, like, big."

"If I could recommend, sir, the Montcharet de Clairenbon."

Taylor jumped in. "That's Daddy's favourite."

I tried to look authoritative. "Well, if it's good enough for Dr. Hoskin, I'm sure it's good enough for us. I mean me. But maybe you could bring an extra glass."

"Certainly, sir," the waiter replied. "I'm sure the wine will be to your liking."

I'm surprised at the number of interruptions that come up when you're supposed to be having a romantic dinner. Somebody always seems to come by to fill a glass, or add a knife, or take away a spoon. Still, it was a lovely meal. The beef carpaccio was soft as butter, my cheap pasta was very nice, and Dr. Hoskin's favourite wine was a bit bitter at first—in fact, it made my mouth wrinkle up as if I'd been sucking a lemon—but it grew on me as the meal progressed.

Taylor and I talked about everything. I learned about her bratty younger sister, her insufferable older brother, her obnoxious mother and her distinguished father—the one person she seemed to idolize. I found out that she disliked the following items: greasy pizza, pretentious guys, loud TV commercials, expensive gold jewellery, her history teacher, golf, her thin blonde hair, Jerry Seinfeld and nasal hair. Please do not ask how all of these came up in conversation. She did like some things: school, the little Mazda she would get next year, *Friends* reruns, pink soccer cleats and intelligent guys. I assumed that last item included me.

I doubt that Taylor learned that much about me since I was so busy listening to her. It was Maggie's rule number one: be attentive. Besides, I was reluctant to go on at any length about my father the professor and my mother the judge for fear that I'd say something totally ridiculous. I figured out one very important thing that night: an effective lie must be carefully planned and researched, which is why it's so easy to get caught on the quick ones that just slip right out.

I would report at greater length about the conversation if there had not been such interesting non-verbal communication beneath the table. At one point, Taylor slipped off her shoe and began to rub her toe over my right foot. I decided to slip off my shoe and do the same to hers, and all this led to a little foot intermingling below the table while the two of us chatted above the table. In old movies, this is referred to as "footsie," and Maggie had said nothing about it in her rules of "do not grope, manhandle or squeeze," so I figured it was okay. In fact, it can actually become exciting after a while—so much so that I felt a quick stirring just where Taylor's dog had moistened my pants.

Obviously, everything was going very well. We sipped the wine, looked into each other's eyes and played footsie beneath the table. *Mission control: we are locked on target,* I said to myself.

Finally the bill came. The footsie stopped and any stirrings of lust were eliminated by the total: $154, with a tip to come. Dr. Hoskin's wine, all by itself, was $48; add on the carpaccio, a couple of drinks, my pasta and Taylor's salmon, one dessert and a couple of coffees—well, the total would have bought a lot of Big Macs.

Taylor opened her purse and handed me sixty dollars. "Will this cover my share?" she asked. And I could have said, honestly, that another twenty would be more like it, but I ran the numbers through my brain and figured that my hundred, with my dad's ten and Taylor's sixty would just cover it, with the tip. Nothing to spare—but why would I need any more?

So we stumbled out of Rayburn's poor but happy, and probably a little drunk.

I haven't mentioned that I don't drink very much. I wish I could say this was a matter of principle, but mostly it has to do with poverty. Sometimes Jeremy and I will grab a beer from his fridge; sometimes my family will let me have a drink at a party; sometimes my aunt Betty will serve me wine when we all go to visit at her place. But I'm not a big drinker. I am underage, slightly, and never really felt the urge to sit around and toss back a two-four while watching a ball game. That's just not me.

So when I drink, it hits me pretty hard. A beer or a glass of wine makes me happy, two make me a bit silly, three make me a bit giddy and four . . . well, I'd never had four drinks before.

Maybe that's why I was having a little trouble with my feet as we left the restaurant—something about placing them on the pavement seemed to require special concentration.

"Do you feel okay?" Taylor asked. Her blue eyes looked at me with wonderful, loving consideration.

"Oh, great," I said, "never better. Just a little dizzy, is all. Must have gotten up too fast."

Taylor smiled and put her arm around me, helping me over the last few steps. I put my arm around her, helping myself to a wonderful touch of her waist, and then kept my arm right where it was. She was so warm, so soft, so wonderful.

Ahmed pulled up in the limo. In a second, he had popped around to open the rear passenger door for us.

"And was the restaurant to your liking?" he asked.

"Very lickable," I replied. "Most lickable meal I've ever licked."

This struck me as remarkably funny, perhaps the wittiest line I had ever delivered in my entire life. That Ahmed didn't get it, and Taylor didn't even giggle, did not stop my appreciation of my own humour.

"Lickable, get it?" I said.

Taylor slid into the car and I bounced in beside her. There was an almost imperceptible change in her at this point. She made no effort to take my hand or restore physical contact or otherwise re-establish the wonderful romance that had been developing in the restaurant.

I knew better than to be aggressive. *Do not grope, manhandle or squeeze*, Maggie had written. *Do not push the Ultimate Goal*. But here we were, in the back of a limo, after a fine, romantic dinner. Surely this was not a time for things to cool down; surely it was time for me to do something.

"A little more champagne, Taylor?" I asked. "Why let it go to waste?"

"I think I've had enough," she replied, "but you go ahead."

"Well, don't mind if I do," I said. Then I filled my glass with the dregs of the champagne, took a large sip and returned my eyes to Taylor.

That is when I first became aware of the problem. Taylor's eyes, in addition to being beautiful, are ordinarily on a straight line. But when I looked at them now, her left eye seemed to be raised up just a little. Then her nose seemed to be moving, just slightly, over towards the left. I blinked. Now both eyes and her nose were moving, and her mouth too, like a real-life painting by Picasso.

"Alan, are you all right?" Taylor asked. "You look pale."

She reached out and touched my face with a most wonderful, gentle hand. I reached up to take her hand in mine, then kissed it very gently. I looked up again and her face was still moving, but not as much as before.

"Oh, I'm good," I said. "It's just been such a wonderful evening."

"For me, too," she said, cuddling against me.

There we sat, in the back of the limousine, cheek to cheek, hand in hand. It was one of those marvellous, romantic moments—or it should have been a marvellous, romantic moment except for a minor problem.

Ahmed was driving the limousine along a windy, undulating road. The twists and turns pushed Taylor and me together—a very nice thing, I should add—but the rises and falls in the road led to a certain wooziness. I felt as if I was in an ocean liner rolling on the high seas, and my stomach, filled with remnants of carpaccio, pasta and wine, began to roll with those seas.

This would have been okay, I supposed, if only everything else had stood still. But now the doorhandles and liquor cabinet and armrest buttons all began dancing up and down. My throat felt very dry, so I finished the last bit of champagne.

"Alan, are you . . .?"

Taylor did not have a chance to finish, because I *was* drunk.

I was sick-to-my-stomach drunk. As that last bit of champagne fizzed down to my stomach, it set off an explosion. I had never felt such a bomb go off in my gut ever before in my life, but the blast was enormous and instantaneous. In less than a second, every-thing—everything!—began rushing upward from my stomach, burning its way into my mouth.

I lurched forward, looking desperately for some place to aim the explosion that was about to come from my mouth. I tried to open the door but couldn't find the handle; I tried to open the window but couldn't find the button. I looked at Taylor's purse as the spew hit the back of my throat. *No!* I told myself. *Not that!*

But my solution was right in front of me—the shiny silver urn that held our champagne. I threw the empty bottle to the floor, bent forward and deposited my entire evening—my entire life—in a dozen convulsive heaves.


When I dared to look over, I saw that Taylor had pressed herself against the door and opened the window for air. She was certainly not looking my way, but must have felt my eyes on her.

Not really looking at me, she said, "Could you ask your driver to take me home?"

So there we were at the end of the night. Taylor's light blonde hair blowing in the breeze, her eyes off somewhere in the distance, her mind thinking God knows what. And there was I, holding a wine cooler full of vomit, my pants stained by dog drool, my dad's blazer dribbled with wine. It was not a picture for Rembrandt or Picasso.

After Taylor left, Ahmed came around to my side of the limo and looked into the wine cooler.

"The food was not to your liking," he said, taking the cooler and dumping the contents on the Hoskins' lawn.

"Not to my liking, no," I grunted.

He drove quickly through the streets to get to my house. By now, the dizziness was gone and the embarrassment was sinking in. I felt miserable. No, *miserable* is too mild a word. I felt a misery unknown to me previously in this life, a desolation so deep and so terrible that I wondered if I should ask Ahmed to simply roll the limo over my body and put an end to it all.

I did not get a chance to ask him.

We were outside my house and I stumbled from the limo. Ahmed was holding the wine cooler in his arms and I wondered, for a moment, if he wanted me to wash it out.

"You were great, Ahmed," I told him.

Ahmed beamed at me. "In that case, sir, I would very much like to receive my fifty dollars. Cash or credit card will be fine."

# 15

# No More Wallowing

"So what are you gonna do?" Jeremy asked. We were back at Starbucks, drinking coffee, staring at the dripping rain outside.

"Wallow," I said.

"What's that?" Jeremy asked, pricking up his ears.

"Wallow in despair," I explained, "like pigs wallow in mud. I'm going to try to pretend I love despair, that I enjoy being shunned by everyone in school, that I don't mind making a fool of myself in front of the girl of my dreams. All thanks to you."

"Me?" He shrugged. His cappuccino left a white moustache on his upper lip. Very uncool, I thought.

"Yeah. You're the guy who always says 'Go for it.' You're the guy who put the champagne in the limo."

"C'mon, Al," he whined. "You're being ungrateful."

I sighed. "I don't even know why I'm sitting here having a coffee with you."

"Maybe because you don't have any other friends," he suggested.

I groaned. "You have to rub that in, don't you?"

"No charge," he replied. "All I told you to do is exactly what I do. The champagne would have worked like a charm if you hadn't—"

I cut him off with a nasty look.

"Well, it works with the St. Hilda's girls. I mean, they spread like butter."

"Would you stop talking like that," I whispered. "Things are bad enough, but if anybody heard you . . ."

In fact, there were very few people who could have heard him. The school crowd had moved over to a new Starbucks, on 13th

Street, so this one had a more adult population. Like most adults, they were generally indifferent to teenagers.

The only exception to this adult population was an Asian girl sitting at a table by the windows. She was reading a book as she sipped what looked to be a frappuccino. The girl was wearing a sweatsuit, but otherwise looked mighty nice.

I guess the girl must have felt me looking at her, the way people can tell even across a big room that someone's eyes are focussed entirely on them. She looked up from her book and stared back at me.

I panicked. God, she must think I'm a pervert. She'll have me arrested for . . . aggressive looking.

Then the most amazing thing happened. She didn't give me the usual eyeball brush-off, the expression that said keep-your-aggressive-eyes-off-me-you-jerk. She smiled.

"Hey, Jeremy," I said.

"What?"

"That girl over there, she smiled at me."

"The old bag?"

"No, the Asian girl. The cute one."

"Smiled at you?" he said, amazed. "Al, you sure you're not hallucinating?"

"No, she smiled . . . at me." I looked around to check the geometry. She was there, the smile was directed across here, but there was nobody else at spot X, so by triangulation and elimination . . . "Yeah, she smiled at me."

"So what are you gonna do?" Jeremy asked. It was the same question he'd started with.

"Make my move," I said, getting to my feet.

Now I won't pretend I wasn't scared. In fact, I was terrified. I had never before made "a move," or at least made a move without practice and coaching beforehand. But now I had reached a place so low, so forlorn, so without hope that nothing I did made any difference. I had a lousy reputation and no prospects. All the girls at my school had already written me off, and they hadn't yet learned about my upchucking in the limo. I was already at zero. When the limo story got out, I would be in minus numbers, if that were possible. So what did it matter? What did anything matter?

So I walked over to the girl's table, my brain fumbling through Maggie's instructions and anything I could think of to start a conversation. *Look at her eyes,* I told myself. *Smile. Be funny. Don't be too aggressive.*

And find a hook. I couldn't just sit down and say that I saw her smiling at me; I needed something . . . something . . . the book. I recognized the book.

"You know," I said, stopping just across from her. *Be confident,* I told myself. "I loved that book, too."

She looked up at me. "You did?"

"I did, really," I told her, in my most sincere voice. The truth was something a little less than that. It was a novel by Michael O'Brien, whose last book had turned into a pretty good movie, but I'd never actually seen this particular book in my life. So maybe *loved* was a bit strong, but it seemed to be the right thing to say. When you're tossing out an opening line, truth is the last thing to worry about.

"I saw you smiling while you were reading," I told her. "You must be near the end." Another slick line, I told myself. Surely any book would have something to smile about near the end.

"No, I'm not that far," she said. "Is it good?"

"You'll love it," I said. Nothing is so certain as total ignorance. "It's when . . . well, I don't want to spoil it for you. But I know you'll like the ending." I hesitated. "Would it be okay if I sit down?" Now that was polite, that was respectful. I was so impressed with myself, surely she'd be impressed too.

"Oh, fine," she said, smiling.

Made it! Conversation: going. Seat: taken. Girl: interested. Now I just had to keep it moving. "Did you see the movie of his last book—what did they call it?"

"*Patterns of Innocence,*" she said. "It was so wonderful."

"That's what I thought, too. It's why I got the new book."

"Me too," she said, her face brightening with an enormous smile. Every tooth was perfect. "They make us read such dull stuff at the college."

I choked. College. *College!* I should have known she was older. I should have been able to see it. She was probably, like, twenty and here I was trying to use pickup lines. Part of me said, *Time to retreat,* but part of me said, *Your BS has worked so far; keep trying.* I went with the second part.

"You're absolutely right," I told her, "but nobody's got the guts to say that."

"Well, I'm in computer science, so I guess it's easy for me to say first-year English is boring. What about you?"

I could have told her the truth at that point. I could have said, *I'm just a pimply-faced teenager in his third year at Regis High School; I'm just a pathetic mass of adolescent flesh that doesn't have a chance with a girl like you.* I could have said that, but those weren't the words that came out of my mouth.

"English lit," I sighed. I tried to make it a wistful sigh.

Okay, so I don't know much about wistful sighs. But our English teacher, Mrs. Grunweld, kept on heaving wistful sighs when she talked about Keats and Shelley. Someday I must read Keats or Shelley and find out what all the sighing is about.

"You must do a lot of reading," she said. The expression on her face seemed full of some emotion, maybe admiration. It was enough to make me puff up.

"I try to keep up. It's hard to find time to read new stuff, like this book."

"But you did read it, uh . . . oh, I don't know your name."

"I'm Alan," I said, putting out my hand. They always shake hands in movies. When Hugh Grant meets Julia Roberts, or whomever, he always shakes hands.

"I'm Rochelle," she said, shaking my hand. "It's like Rachel with an *o.*"

"That's a beautiful name," I said. I meant it, too. So maybe I was lying a lot about me, but I wasn't lying at all about her.

Rochelle blushed. "You're not trying to pick me up or something, are you?"

Now I blushed. "Me? Pick you up?" I asked. It was the old double-question thing, to make me sound kind of innocent. *Now what would Hugh Grant do?* I asked myself. Hugh Grant would be charming, sweet and honest. "Actually, I am."

"Am what?" she asked.

"I am trying to pick you up. I love your smile. I love that you read Michael O'Brien. And I love that you love the book I love." Okay, the last bit was over the top, but the effect was perfect.

She smiled. Her bright eyes looked into mine.

I smiled back. "So I'm sorry about trying to pick you up, which I know is impolite, but there really is no polite way to do it, is there? I mean, I see a perfect girl sitting here, reading a great book, and I could just let the moment go or I could, as Keats once said, go for it and make a fool of myself."

"Did Keats say that?"

"No, but he must have thought it."

"You're funny, Alan."

"Thank you. Usually I'm very serious," I told her, "but I'm working on being funny."

"I kind of like you the way you are," she said. It was the most honest, sincere sentence that I had ever heard in my life. It almost made me feel bad for lying and exaggerating as much as I had. But another part of me was ready to jump up and shout, "Hey, this hot girl likes me. Likes MEEE!"

Behind me I heard a cough, and then a faint "Excuse me." I looked up to see Jeremy with a peculiar expression on his face.

"Al, sorry, but I'm going to go."

"That's okay," I told him, "so go. Go." I could have added a third "Go" but I thought that would be a bit too much.

"See you tomorrow," he said, heading off.

"Professor Jones's class, first thing," I called after him, adding just a bit more to my story.

"You have Jones for first-year lit?" Rochelle asked.

*Oh no!* Who would have thought there really was a Professor Jones up at the college? "Well, yeah."

"I hear Jones is tough," she said. "A tough marker."

"I don't know," I replied, an honest remark. "He must like me, I mean, he must like what I write, my essays and stuff." Ooh, that did not sound too impressive.

Rochelle gave me a thoughtful look. "Maybe you're just really good at literature." She looked at me with these wonderful bright eyes, so full of appreciation. How could I tell her the truth?

"Well, I'm not sure about that," I replied, "but I do like Keats and Shelley."

# 16

# Still More Advice

LYING IS TOUGH WORK. Especially if it's a fairly large, ongoing lie. It's one thing to tell your parents "I was over at Joe's house" when you actually went cruising with Rocco Vanzetti in his souped-up Honda. You won't get pressed for details about what you did, and they're unlikely to call Joe or actually spot you roaring down 8th Street in the car. A simple one-shot, one-evening lie—that's the easy kind.

But a large, ongoing lie requires work and careful research. If I was a first-year student at the college, where did I live? At home. Why? To save money. What else did I take besides Professor Jones's English class? Well, I had no idea. If we were playing twenty questions, I'd survive maybe three.

Of course, Rochelle wasn't grilling me while we sat at Starbucks. If the conversation turned towards school, I'd listen hard, nod my head and sympathize. Then I'd talk about the weather, or the government's latest idiocy, or some book I'd heard about on TV. My best defence, of course, is that I'm a good listener. It worked with Mel, it worked with Taylor and it was working with Rochelle.

But when I got home, clutching Rochelle's phone number written hastily on a scrap of paper, I knew I had to do some work. That's what the Internet is for, isn't it? Just log on to the college website, check out the tuition fees, residences and first-year courses.

Whoa! One look at the fees and I could see why I was living at home. First year, I'd be taking a math course—the easy one, Math 103; a language course—maybe Italian because it's so poetic; English with good old Jones; and two electives. I picked Philosophy

102, a consideration of moral dilemmas. That would be good. And Art History just to round myself out. Keats, Shelley, Plato and Picasso . . . a great combination.

"You BS artist," Jeremy said when he called me that night. "I could hear you lying through your teeth. How did you pull that off?"

"With panache," I told him.

"You don't know what panache is."

"Yes, I do," I replied, smiling into the phone, "because I'm a first-year English major with a big vocabulary. And I got a book, *Thirty Days to a Brilliant Vocabulary*."

"She's going to see right through you."

"Sooner or later," I admitted. "But if I can make it later, maybe I'll do okay along the way."

"I have to hand it to you, Al," he said. "You've got *cojones*."

"I already knew that," I told him, "but what I really need is brains."

The two of us agreed that Maggie need not know about Rochelle. I'm certain that a suggestion like "use lies to pretend you're something that you're not" would never be on any of her advice lists. Besides, I was in a territory where Maggie couldn't give me any good advice. My problem wasn't in impressing Rochelle, or paying appropriate attention to such a wonderful girl, it was in keeping Rochelle from discovering the pathetic guy I really was.

So far, I was doing just fine. The next day I made a phone call to the house she shared with a bunch of girls. Once I got past a room-mate who seemed to be suffering brain damage, Rochelle was delighted that I'd called. I offered a Friday-night movie date; she came back with a Friday-night *play*.

"It's a Beckett play," she said. "I'm surprised Dr. Jones didn't tell you to go."

"Ah, Beckett," I replied, trying to sound knowledgeable. "Very interesting stuff, those Beckett plays." I kept searching through my memory banks trying to come up with something about a guy named Beckett. Didn't some British king chop off his head? Must be a different Beckett. Must be the kind of play they don't do as a made-for-TV movie.

"Then we can go out after," she said, "and maybe get a drink or something."

A *drink,* I thought and shivered. After my date with Taylor, I may never drink again. "Yeah, that would be great."

"And good luck on your quiz tomorrow," Rochelle added.

I was dumbfounded. "Quiz?"

"Yeah. Dr. Jones is giving you a quiz on the Romantic poets. One of my roommates is in your class and she told me all about it."

Bells were ringing in my head—danger bells. "Oh, right, *that* quiz. Well, I'm more than ready. I know 'La Belle Dame Sans Merci' like my left hand." That wonderful simile was possible only after significant Internet research. If I ever had to meet Rochelle's roommate, I'd have to read about every book and poem on the course.

"Well, good luck with the quiz. See you Friday about seven."

Okay, I admit I was getting a little nervous about all this. A roommate in my non-existent English class; a quiz on Romantic poets I had never read. But I wasn't ready to give up. I had no alternatives, really, and this thing with Rochelle was still going just fine—if you ignored a few potential glitches. Besides, there was her promise that we'd go out for a drink "or something." Wasn't "or something" exactly what I'd been looking for? Wasn't the Ultimate Goal the point of all this?

I mentioned to my parents that I'd be out on a date on Friday, and they seemed to respond with their usual generalized curiosity and wholesome advice. My mother is so hopelessly supportive of everything I do that I half expected her to offer me twenty bucks to cover the costs. But it was my father who surprised me.

Thursday night, he came up behind me in the computer/TV/ everything room. Thankfully I was checking out Samuel Beckett, playwright, on the Internet rather than some porn site.

"Sorry to interrupt, Al," my dad said. "I can see you're studying."

"Yeah, got a major test on this Beckett guy on Friday."

"Right," he said, standing awkwardly at the door. "Mind if I talk to you for a minute?"

This was truly strange, I thought. My dad never asked if he could talk to me. By and large, he didn't talk to me unless he had to, and when he did, he never asked permission. But there he was, wearing one of those "dad" sweaters that my mother keeps buying him, shifting his weight from one foot to another.

"No problem," I told him.

Dad kept looking at the floor or the computer screen, as if he were afraid to meet my eyes. For a second, I had this awful thought: my parents are going to get a divorce and he's come to tell me. That must be it—just like on TV, except we didn't have any sucky music in the background.

"Al, it's probably a little late to talk to you about this . . .," he began.

"Is it you and Mom?" I asked, my voice all scratchy.

"Well, Mom and I have been talking," he said, "and she thought I should talk to you about it."

By now I was really worried. "About what?"

"About, uh, well, sex."

I let out a major sigh of relief. This wasn't "the divorce talk"; it was "the birds and the bees talk." I leaned back in my chair. "Well, we started talking about that in school about grade three," I told him.

My dad looked more embarrassed. "I know. But your mom and I notice that you're going out a lot these days, and we thought, I mean, your mom thought I should talk to you about . . . protection."

"Protection?" My mind shifted to Val Halvorsen and his goons. I could use some protection from those guys.

"It's just that, sooner or later . . . and I hope it's later . . . you're going to be, uh, sexually active."

"Well, I hope so," I said. Suddenly I felt very relaxed. My dad was so nervous that he managed to make me feel calm.

"And you know there are a lot of diseases you can get from, well, doing it with people you don't know . . ."

"I've seen pictures," I told him, which was true. We had a video in our biology class that was so graphic it would make any sensible person give up sex forever. Of course, teenagers aren't all that sensible. Maybe if there were pictures of gonorrhea infections on beer bottles, like those cancer pictures on cigarette packs, it would give us a whole generation of celibates.

"Anyhow, I just wanted to tell you to be careful and give you this," he said. He handed me a foil packet—a genuine lubricated condom. "And there's a whole box in the downstairs bathroom, just in case you need more."

*Wow,* I thought, *my parents must think I'm quite the stud muffin.* My mouth dropped open.

"Not that this gives you permission, you know. I mean, it's not that we think sex before you make a serious commitment is a good idea."

My father seemed to be at a loss for words at this point, so I decided to help him out. "No, no, this is, like, just in case."

"Right, just in case." And with that, my dad left.

*Just in case,* I repeated to myself. *Just in case I get laid* . . . and maybe it'll be tomorrow night!

# 17

# A Little Culture Can Be Just Enough

OKAY, SO MY BRAIN was kind of rushing ahead. Just because I had a condom didn't mean I'd actually get to use it. I mean, I had been carrying a Trojan around in my wallet so long that the thing must be turning to dust. But now, courtesy of my parents, I had a brand-new condom—a lubricated condom—and access to a whole box of lubricated condoms!

Thoughts like that can make a guy feel overwhelmed by parental affection. It was almost enough to make up for the fact that the girls at my school still looked on me like some kind of unpleasant crustacean, that the girls at St. Agnes would soon learn I couldn't hold my liquor, that the gardener at the Hoskin mansion was probably grossed out by what he found on his lawn, and that my latest attempt at seduction was based on fraud and outright lies. *At least,* I said to myself, *at least I have protection.*

And thanks to the Internet, I had *information*:

*Samuel Beckett. b. Dublin 1906, moved to Paris 1937, d. Paris, 1989, best known for the absurdist drama* Waiting for Godot, *winner of the Nobel Prize in 1969. Beckett's literary works reduce basic existential problems to their essential elements—the frustration of life; the individual's sense of loneliness, despair and alienation; the impossibility of establishing real communication with others; the mystery of identity. His works effectively depict the aridity of modern life.*

By Friday night, I had looked up *existential* and *alienation*, so I was ready. Okay, I didn't understand either of them, but I was ready enough. I practised saying the word *aridity* so it didn't come out sounding too strange. I even reviewed Maggie's notes before I left the house, just in case I'd forgotten anything in my general enthusiasm. I had everything a guy might need before a really hot date with a really hot girl.

At 7:05 I was knocking on the door to Rochelle's shared house. Actually, I could have been knocking on the door ten minutes earlier, but I figured that early was uncool. Above all, I wanted to seem cool.

The door was opened by a roommate who might have been Hannah the Honker's older sister. "Chelle is almost ready," she announced casually, then strolled off to another room in the house.

Minutes later, Rochelle came out of the bathroom, bringing with her a wave of perfume and shower steam. She looked magnificent: dark hair tied back; an all-black outfit that matched my all-black sort-of-Jean-Paul-Sartre look, but hers was perfectly fitted. Rochelle was a thin girl who looked like an exotic model for Versace or Gucci. In a very different way, she may have been more beautiful than Taylor Hoskin. Rochelle was so beautiful that looking at her made my teeth hurt.

Really.

"You're incredible," I said. My eyes were on her eyes, but I caught all the rest.

"You think?" she said, smiling.

"Oh yeah. If Samuel Beckett had ever met you, he wouldn't have wasted his time waiting for Godot."

I thought that was a pretty good line; kind of an artsy, literary joke suitable for a first-year Eng. lit. student.

Rochelle gave me a wan smile. That was a new word for me too—*wan*. It's a kind of appreciative, gentle smile; the kind of smile that women would have given to Keats and Shelley.

Rochelle shouted something to the disappeared roommate, and then the two of us headed out the door. Rochelle's hair glowed in the setting sun, her eyes sparkled, the dust-filled air seemed to glow in anticipation of the night to come.

"My roommate says that Dr. Jones is coming to the play tonight."

I gulped. *Stay cool,* I told myself. *No reason to panic. Say something witty and in control.*

"Well, maybe I can read his eyes and see how I did on the poets quiz."

Rochelle gave me a strange look for a moment, then it passed and she started talking about a test she'd had in database applications, whatever those are. I kept trying to turn the conversation back to my newly acquired knowledge of Samuel Beckett and his theatre in Montparnasse. I even thought of pretending that I'd once visited Montparnasse, but for someone who hasn't even been to Parnassus, New Jersey, I figured that would be too tough to carry off.

The best thing about the campus theatre is that it's really cheap, cheaper than a movie. Of course, Rochelle offered to pay her own way, but I said something about all the money I saved by living at home, so I bought her ticket. *Gallant,* I said to myself. Going to a play written in Paris, I should certainly be *gall-ant,* as they say in French.

We were moving from the ticket line into the lobby of Crispin Hall when I was stopped by a familiar face . . . in fact, by two familiar faces.

"Alan?" I heard. The big rising tone at the end told me that she couldn't believe my presence here, of all places.

"Uh, Maggie," I replied. *Stay cool,* I told myself. *No confusion, just be gracious. Be gall-ant.*

She looked from me to Rochelle and then back to me. "Well, Alan, I see you're making good progress all by yourself. Do I get introduced?"

"Sure. Uh, Maggie, this is, uh, Rochelle." For just a second I stumbled over her name. That was the same moment that sweat began to pop out of my forehead. I turned to Rochelle to explain, "Maggie is, uh, a friend . . . from high school."

"Hello," Rochelle said, perfectly poised, as always.

"And this is Braden, Maggie's, uh, friend."

Braden smiled his perfect smile, that Colgate-white-strip straight-tooth smile that always made my own teeth turn yellow with envy. Then he reached forward and shook Rochelle's hand, effortlessly, as if he'd been shaking hands with beautiful girls all his life.

Maggie just stared at me. "I didn't know you liked modern plays," she said.

"Well, uh"—I apologize for all these *uh*'s, but I kept on trying to buy time with unintelligible grunts and groans—"I, uh, I had a bit of an overload with Keats and Shelley lately."

"And what are you studying, Rochelle?" Braden asked. The words slipped off his tongue so easily that I had a hunch he'd used it to pick up a hundred girls in a hundred different places.

"Oh, computers. I'm just in first year," Rochelle said, quite modestly, I thought.

"I'm thinking of going into computers myself," Braden said to her. "Maybe you could tell me a little about the program."

And then, I'm not sure how he did it, but somehow he steered Rochelle to one side so they could talk together. It was a pretty slick move, getting my girlfriend to himself for a few minutes, so naturally I wanted to kill him. I was (a) jealous and (b) afraid. The jealousy makes obvious sense, but I was also worried that Braden might somehow blow my whole cover story.

"It's okay, Alan," Maggie said. "Braden just likes to flirt with pretty girls. And your new friend really is quite beautiful."

"Yeah, well. She's pretty special in lots of ways," I mumbled. I kept my eye on Braden's back, using telepathy to beam into his brain: *Don't talk about school, don't tell her we're in high school, don't don't don't.*

"I'm kind of surprised that she'd go out with a high-school kid," Maggie added.

"Well, it's kind of a miracle," I told her, smiling my very best smile. I suppose I could have told her about Alan the first-year English major, but I had a hunch that massive lying to a possible girlfriend would not rate too high in Maggie's eyes.

Fortunately, the please-be-seated bell went off before Maggie could ask me any more or Braden could spill the beans. I breathed a very real sigh of relief.

"Well, we better find our seats," I said, reclaiming Rochelle by taking her arm. "Nice seeing you, Maggie . . . and you too, Braden." The perspiration on my forehead suddenly seemed to cool as we walked away.

"Maybe we can meet you after the play," Braden suggested, looking more at Rochelle than at me.

I pretended a sudden deafness and guided Rochelle into the theatre. I'd sooner perform a coronary bypass on myself with a kitchen knife than meet them after the play.

"Was Braden trying to put moves on you?" I asked, trying not to sound too nervous about it.

She laughed. "No, he just wondered about the courses I was taking. That's all. And what about that girl Maggie? What about her?"

"Oh, nothing," I said. "It's just that, well, Maggie was an old girl-friend once and, uh, I guess I'm still kind of awkward about that."

"You are just too sensitive," she said, squeezing my hand. "Don't be embarrassed. I could tell you were pretty experienced with girls."

*Experienced with girls!* Whoa! My experience amounted to three sets of instructions and two actual dates, but somehow Rochelle had been impressed. She thought I was sensitive. She thought I was experienced. Maybe she thought I was hot!

*Control yourself, Alan,* I told myself. I'd just had a narrow escape; there was no sense thinking that I was home free now. I held Rochelle's hand as we went down the left aisle and found our seats in the second row. Maggie and Braden, thank God, were seated five rows behind us. Two rows in front of us, on stage, was a bare set with a window and a table.

"Not a very elaborate set," Rochelle commented.

I was ready. I had studied up on this. "Beckett liked to use sparse settings. He was making a statement about the aridity of modern life."

"Ah," she replied.

I had a hunch she didn't know what "aridity of modern life" meant, and neither did I, but I had memorized the phrase, practised the pronunciation and was determined to use it at least once.

After the lights dimmed, two actors named Hamm and Clov started going on and on about, well, maybe it was about the aridity of modern life. After a while, it even began to make a little sense. Maybe, I thought, maybe I really should become an English major. Then again, maybe I should pass high-school English first.

Now before I get to the scary part, let me tell you about the best part. Rochelle. All the time we were watching this play, part of me was very aware that she was beside me, warm, beautiful, and touching my arm with hers. I was very aware of her skin, the smoothness of her skin, and the wonderful smell of her perfume. And there were times when I'd look over at her and see her profile, those perfect features, those dark eyes intent on the play. There were times when I said to myself, *Al, you're falling in love*. But I had to snap out of that. I had to concentrate on goal one. Falling in love would be kind of a bonus, like the extra set of scissors they give you when you buy the $129 set of knives on the Home Shopping Channel.

At last the play ended, and the actors got a big round of applause. I thought it was well deserved because the dialogue didn't make much sense but they managed to make it sound like it meant something. Rochelle was clapping enthusiastically, so naturally I joined her. I was cool, but not too cool to applaud.

When we turned to leave, I saw that Maggie and Braden were already going up the aisle. I decided we'd be in no rush; in fact, the last thing I wanted was to catch up with them. I made a point of looking under my seat, trying to find where my program had dropped. I told Rochelle that I might need it for my English class, so that blew a minute or two—enough time to get Maggie and Braden right out of the theatre.

We were in the clear, almost.

"Oh, look," Rochelle said as we got to the aisle, "there's Dr. Jones."

A brief moment of panic. What did Dr. Jones look like: grey hair, dark hair, dreadlocks; moustache, beard, glasses, knobby nose, what? I stared in the same general direction as Rochelle.

"Don't you want to talk to her about the play?" Rochelle asked.

*Her! Dr. Jones is a HER!* No wonder Rochelle had looked at me strangely back at the house when I called her a him.

"Well, I, uh . . .," I replied, a kind of multi-word grunt.

Without waiting for an answer, Rochelle marched up the steps to a middle-aged woman with her hair pulled back into a ponytail. There she was—Dr. Jones, my prof. Dr. Jones, the professor who should have been marking my non-existent Romantic poets quiz.

A bold front, I decided, was the only front to put up.

"Dr. Jones," I said in a loud voice, "you said you'd be here."

The woman turned and looked at me with a piercing stare. I cringed. I could see her studying my face, wondering who on earth I was.

"Yes, yes, it's nice to see you here, uh . . ."

"Alan," I filled in. She must have figured I was one of three hundred students whom she ought to recognize. Bonus.

Dr. Jones smiled. "Of course, Alan. I'm glad you took my advice and came to see the play. Wasn't it wonderful?"

"Oh yes," I said. "I think the actor who played Clov was especially good. And the whole play, well, it really captured the aridity of modern life."

"Yes," she said. "It certainly made me wish I'd brought a water bottle."

I gave a little laugh and made a mental note to look up *aridity* when I got home. I mean, when a word like that creeps into your vocabulary, you almost have an obligation to know what it means.

Dr. Jones went off with some man who might have been Mr. Dr. Jones and seemed somewhat relieved not to have to talk to me any more. Of course I was equally relieved not to have to talk to her. I'd pretty much exhausted my bank of memorized literary phrases.

As we walked out, Rochelle whispered, "I don't think she recognized you." I could feel her hot breath on my ear and, I confess, it started to get me excited.

"Guess not," I replied, smiling conspiratorially.

"These profs have so many students," Rochelle said. "I read that one economics prof has almost two thousand students. The TAs do all the work, but still they feel kind of guilty."

*What's a TA?* I asked myself. *Is it like T&A? No, not that,* I silently replied. All this was part of an extended internal dialogue that took maybe two seconds. Paralyzed by indecision or stupidity or both, I decided to smile and be agreeable.

"So what did you think?" I asked her. Time to go back to Maggie's list: focus on the girl. No opinion is as interesting to the girl as her own.

"Well, I kind of . . . to tell you the truth"—she paused—"I think it mostly sailed over my head. I mean I liked it, but, well . . ."

"Hey, can I tell you the truth?"

She nodded, smiling that wonderful smile.

"Mostly it sailed way over my head too."

And then the most amazing thing happened. We started giggling, out in the corridor of Crispin Hall, giggling like two kids caught with their hands in the cookie jar. And then I took her hand, and Rochelle kind of angled her head, and I kind of looked down at her—and we were both still laughing—and I kissed her. It was a funny kiss, that first one, full of giggles and smiles, but quite wonderful.

And then there was the second kiss, and that one was serious. I took hold of her with one arm, and she pulled me right up against her body, and our mouths came together in a serious, serious kiss.

When we pulled back, I think we both became aware of people staring at us. Not that there's anything wrong with kissing a hot girl in public, but it gets a bit awkward when people stare. Rochelle pulled away somewhat and I took my hand off her back but I couldn't let go of her hand.

"Sorry," I told her. "I got carried away."

"I like it when you get carried away," she whispered back.

*Oh my god!* I screamed to myself. *This is a dream. Don't slap me, I don't want to wake up. This is a fantasy turned into real life. This is a Harlequin romance. This is a daytime soap opera. This is my every dream come true . . .* just don't let it end.

# 18

# Another Bill Arrives, and More Advice

THERE ARE NASTY aspects to real life. I find that they come back periodically to slap you in the face, just when you need them the least. I was still floating in a romantic dream world on Monday morning when Maggie came to my locker and said she wanted to see me at lunch.

"A consultation?" I asked.

"The April bill," she replied flatly. "I'm just a bit late with it."

Needless to say, I wasn't looking forward to our meeting. There was, I suppose, the iffy question of whether I owed her five dollars for a date that I had set up entirely by myself. On the other hand, it was her advice that got me the date, so maybe she deserved the fee. Or maybe she'd have more advice for me. Surely I was getting to the stage where I should know just a little bit more.

Maggie was waiting by herself when I got to the cafeteria. She had her glasses back on and was looking serious.

"Hey," I said, sitting down.

"Hey yourself," she replied. "Looks like you're doing very well on your own steam. And just when I found a girl who thought the whole elevator-grope thing was a laugh."

"You did?" I replied. "You found me another girl?"

"Yeah, but I'll hold her in reserve. We've got to get the payment issues cleaned up first."

"Right."

Maggie slid an envelope across the table.

**Maggie McPherson Consulting**
Statement of Account for April


Project: Alan

| | |
|---|---|
| Website revamp | $10.00 |
| First date, Taylor Hoskin | 25.00 |
| Email editing | 10.00 |
| Counselling, aversion therapy | <u>30.00</u> |
| | |
| Total for April | $75.00 |
| | |
| Installment now due | $75.00 |

Your patronage and prompt payment is always appreciated.


"Website revamp?" I asked.

"I had to add meta-tags," she replied flatly.

"Ah, yes, of course." I'll have to ask Rochelle what meta-tags are.

You'll notice that I didn't charge you for Rochelle," Maggie said matter-of-factly. "I debated whether or not our agreement covered extraneous dates, but decided to give you a break. Obviously you're doing well."

"Yeah, thanks, I am," I blurted. I felt more than a little stupid, and was probably blushing some splendid shade of red.

"And if you want to call this whole thing off after you pay the bill, well, that's okay with me." Maggie looked up at me through her glasses with a funny expression on her face.

"No, no. I'm not ready yet."

"Well, I could have told you that," Maggie said. "But I find that once guys get a little success in something, they tend to think they're geniuses and can do the rest on their own. The male ego is an extraordinary thing."

"Yeah, right," I agreed, "but with everything going so well with Rochelle I was kind of wondering . . ."

"What to do next?"

"Yeah."

She thought about that for a second. Someplace in the background, a toasted cheese sandwich went sailing through the air. Someplace else, there was a PA announcement for the jazz band rehearsal. But right in front of me, Maggie took off her glasses and smiled at me. "That would go into the next billing period."

"It's okay," I replied. "I need a little advice about . . . third base."

She just shook her head. "Alan, pretty soon you'll get to the point where I can't give you advice any more."

"Yeah," I said, "that would be good. Real good."


I got together with Jeremy after school for the usual guy stuff: a little baseball toss, a little talk about sports and the horrors of Mr. Greer's math class, and a British beer from his dad's basement refrigerator.

"How you doing with that Asian chick?" he asked idly.

I tried to suppress a smile. "Coming along . . . sort of second base."

"Sort of?"

"Okay, second base, hoping for third," I said proudly.

"You sly dog," he said. "Still lying through your teeth and she's falling for it, eh?"

I said nothing.

"Yeah, that's what I figured. It's amazing the crap that girls will fall for. I once told this girl that my dad was a commodore at the yacht club—can you believe that? She swallowed that one, hook, line and sinker. Kept bugging me for a sail on the old yacht, so finally I had to break it off."

"Yeah, I've had to do some studying up on Keats and Shelley to pull off my first-year thing. By the time I get to college, I'll have half the first-year English course already finished."

"So what was she like? I've never been with an Asian girl."

Uh-oh, a direct question. Guys so rarely ask each other direct questions that I wasn't quite ready for it. But the question brought an image of Rochelle into my mind, and then how I felt about Rochelle, and then a kind of heat that spread all over my face.

"Jeez, you're blushing, Al," Jeremy observed. "Must be hot and heavy."

"Well, uh . . ." I cleared my throat. "She's, uh . . . pretty special."

"Excuse me while I go barf," Jeremy said, then burst into laughter. "Sounds like you've got it bad, my boy—*baaad*."

I could feel the heat in my cheeks and figured I was blushing even worse than before.

"I tell you, Al, you've got to get over this romance crap. Yeah, I know, the first girl to give you a serious kiss, or maybe let you cop a feel, and all of a sudden you think you're in love. But it's not love, Al, it's lust. Pure and simple lust."

I wanted to say *no, no it isn't,* but I knew better. Guys don't talk about falling in love. They hardly ever talk about anything important. They talk about sports or cars or school but never, ever about love. Breathe one word of it out loud and the laughter could be heard all over town.

"Al, you gotta take my advice," Jeremy went on. The second British beer makes him wax poetic or philosophical or both. "Girls like direct. You know what I mean? None of this beating around the bush stuff. You gotta be like Clint Eastwood and just go for it."

"Yeah, yeah," I said. It seemed to me I had gotten this advice before, with fairly disastrous results.

"It works, Al," Jeremy said. "I mean, look at me. I'm a pretty ugly guy but I'm dynamite with women. So how come? Some days I ask myself that. Look at this face and this very much un-buff body."

I actually did look at Jeremy. As guys, we almost never looked at each other—it's against the guy code of ethics. You look at a friend only when he's been injured, so you can check out the bruises and scars, or when he's done a truly disgusting fart or has a booger hanging from his nose, so you can make fun of him. But at that second

I looked at Jeremy: the puffy face, the ten-pounds-overweight body, the lips that were always wet with spit. How could anybody find that attractive? I wondered.

"You see," Jeremy said. "Ugly. Verging on repulsive, if I do say so myself, but I still do just fine. It's all in the moves, Al, and the confidence."

"Yeah, I guess it must be," I said.

"Trust me, Al. I know you're going to pretend you're a sensitive guy—jeez, you *are* a sensitive guy—but it's not going to get you laid. You can play Mr. Nice Guy forever, but you'll die a virgin."

I grunted agreement. It's sometimes tough to get guy conversation down in writing because so much of it consists of grunts and laughter.

"Hey," Jeremy said, "I saw something good in some magazine the other day, something that might help you. It's an acronym: KFUG."

"KFUG?"

"Yeah, it stands for Kiss, Feel, Unbutton and Go for it. Girls like a guy with confidence, who shows that he's in control. So remember, KFUG."

I had a hunch that Maggie would not approve of KFUG. I had a hunch that Maggie would not approve of my dissembling to Rochelle. Pretty good word, *dissembling*, which is poetic for lying but sounds so much nicer. Still, I knew Maggie wouldn't like it much and might walk away from the whole project if she knew.

So I kept my mouth shut. I got $75 from the bank, put it in an envelope and went to meet Maggie after school.

"You've got the money?" she asked. That seemed a little crass, even to me, but I guess it's the kind of question lawyers have to ask.

"Here," I said, handing her the envelope.

"Thanks. Now I've got a little bad news on this set of instructions you asked for."

I noticed that she wasn't wearing her glasses today, and something else was different, too. Her braces were gone.

"Hey, you've got teeth," I said.

She shook her head. "So glad you noticed, Al. With subtlety like that, it's amazing that you're doing as well with Rochelle as you are."

"Yeah, well, that's different," I said.

"Anyway, I had to get some help in writing this instruction set, so I got some of the girls together and had to pay for some coffee and dessert."

"How much?"

"Thirty-two dollars and ten cents."

"Jeez, that's a lot of coffee."

"It's the lattes that really cost. Anyway, there's an expense clause in your contract, so I'm just doing a pass-through on the cost."

"Where did you learn all this business talk?"

"From my mother," Maggie snapped, "when I still had one. Anyhow, are we going ahead or what?"

"You didn't tell them about our arrangement, did you?" I asked, suddenly panicked.

"You pay me for confidentiality, as well as counsel. Trust me, Al."

Maggie was the second person to use the "trust me" phrase, but I figured I didn't have much choice in the matter. "In for a penny, in for a pound," says Jeremy's father, which translates into something like "go for it" in the language of ordinary guys.

"Okay, I'll pay, but not until the next billing," I said.

"Fair enough." Then Maggie slid me a plain brown envelope.

**PROJECT: ALAN**
Instruction set 3

Congratulations, Alan, you are nearing your Ultimate Goal. Once again, the basic philosophy is to be patient. "Neither love nor sex can be rushed, both have their own time schedule," to quote one of your team of advisers.

We suspect that most of your information about sex comes from porn videos (you need not admit this publicly). Just to correct some pornography-based inaccuracies that may be cluttering your brain:

1. Most women do not have breasts as large as those you have seen on video; nor do we ordinarily like them to be squeezed or pinched.
2. Real women do not groan, pant or scream with desire while making love; Meg Ryan showed just how silly this concept is in *When Harry Met Sally.*
3. Real women do not particularly idolize your private parts; in truth we are not anxious to touch them, massage them or pretend they are a lollipop; if we consent to do so, consider yourself very, very lucky.
4. There is no magic button anywhere on the female anatomy that leads to instant seduction.

Since we are correcting possible misconceptions, let us offer a remarkable concept: for girls, the most erogenous zone is the brain; all other parts of the body are far down the list. To seduce a girl's brain, we recommend the following:
1. Women love, in descending order, (1) love, (2) compliments, (3) little gifts and (4) chocolate.
2. Always tell the girl how much you love her. This works even better if you really do love her.
3. Regardless of point 2, tell the girl how beautiful/wonderful/unique she is. No matter how beautiful/wonderful/unique a girl may be (trust us, at least one of your advisers is all of these), she is deeply unsure of herself. Tell her how wonderful she is, again and again.
4. Women are unimpressed with your family's wealth, your car, your income potential and the pricey gifts you might want to give us. We do love little gifts. Keep the sportscar; buy chocolates once a week.

As a man (almost), we suspect that you'd like a little technical advice on seduction. A complete run-down would require a book, but we will offer these five tips to help you along:

1. Lips are a very sensitive area. Kiss a lot. Figure 30 minutes of kissing before you try *anything* else. That's 30 *minutes*, not 30 seconds.
2. After that, every girl is different. Some girls like to have their necks nuzzled; some hate it. Some girls like to have their breasts gently touched; some hate it. Look for signs of delight or irritation. If in doubt, ask.
3. Girls take a long time. You may get sexually excited in ten seconds; we may take ten minutes, or ten *hours*. It all depends.
4. As a general principle, gentle is better than rough.
5. Never forget, girls like sex too. But we don't like stupid, clueless men who think that slam-bam-thank-ya-ma'am sex is a guy's reward for dinner out. We don't owe you anything; if you can understand that, you may just reach your Ultimate Goal.

# 19

# I Never Asked for Trouble

MAY IS THE MONTH for lovers. May is the month when you can walk hand in hand through the rain-kissed air, the month when the spring flowers have finally come into bloom, the month when our hidden hearts beat in anticipation of everything to come.

Or, as Jeremy said, May is the month to get laid.

So there I was, on campus, walking Rochelle home from a Hugh Grant movie at the student centre. It was a perfect, perfect May night, with a hint of the just-set sun giving a glow to the sky above Crispin Hall, a handful of stars twinkling over our heads, and a crescent moon looking about as big and beautiful as any moon I'd ever seen. It was the kind of night that Keats or Shelley would have appreciated, the kind of night they must have captured in their poetry. At that very moment, in fact, I vowed to actually read some of it. Nights like this, moments like this, were the reasons why people wrote poetry.

I had a beautiful girl beside me, holding my hand, a girl who thought I was bright, witty and sensitive. She also thought I was a first-year college student, but let's ignore that for now. Let's stick to an image of me, Alan, a mostly gawky-geeky teenager, holding the hand of this goddess under a night sky so romantic that, if life were a musical, I would probably burst out into song.

Rochelle turned and looked into my eyes. "Alan," she sighed.

"Chelle," I whispered back.

We held hands, looking at each other, feeling the moment and our closeness. *This must be falling in love,* I said to myself. *This is what all those songs are about. This is what I always wanted . . .*

I was leaning forward to kiss Rochelle when I heard the first voice.

"Well, look at that. Ain't that Al the pervert?"

"And he's holding hands with a real babe!"

The second voice was vaguely familiar. I turned to look. It was Val Halvorsen.

Just beside Val was Joey McGee, called McGoo by the kids at school because his face looked like some cartoon character's. Next to McGoo was another member of the football squad whose name was Bob or Rob or Blob . . . something like that. Together, they made a very large trio—not so much from a musical, but from an opera. I mean, these guys were big.

"Listen, guys . . .," I began. I knew I had to say something. I knew that my perfect moment with Rochelle was over and that some kind of test had begun. They were pushing me into a fight—a fight I couldn't possibly win—and I had to find some way out without sacrificing too much personal dignity in the process. "How about you go your way and we'll go ours and—"

"Sounds like Al is feeling a little nervous," said McGoo.

"He's sure sweating like a pig," added Blob.

"This guy really *is* a pig," Val joined in. "Just ask my sister."

"Hey, nobody needs this," Rochelle said.

"Uh-oh, looks like his girlfriend is getting a little mad," McGoo said. "Better watch out for the chink."

Now that was getting over the top. I let go of Rochelle's hands and stepped towards them. I had no idea how I was going to handle this, but I knew I didn't want her getting hurt. Somehow I had to shut this down and shut them up.

"Now I never asked for trouble from you guys—" I began again.

"No, but you got trouble, meathead," Val replied. He didn't actually say "meathead"; his level of swearing was a couple notches up from that, referring both to sex and anatomy in ways that were not complimentary. But the words were the easy part. It was the shove that really got to me.

I wasn't quite ready for the shove. Val pushed me off balance and

I went sailing backwards, falling for a second, then catching myself with one hand. I was back on my feet pretty quick.

And then I lost it. I raced at Val, aiming my right fist at his jaw. He deflected it with his arm, as if my punch were about as dangerous as being attacked by a flyswatter. Then somebody—McGoo or the Blob—punched me from the side and I saw stars, not the nice cartoon-style stars but those little sparks that shoot around your vision when you've taken a decent-sized hit.

It only took one more hit to send me to the ground. This punch was to my stomach, and a little follow-through by Val pushed me down to the grass beside the walkway. Now I had shooting stars in my eyes, a burning pain in my gut and a little grass in my mouth.

I rolled to one side, trying to find a way to get up, when I heard a loud crack followed by a scream.

"She kicked me!" McGoo cried, falling beside me on the grass.

I looked up to see Rochelle stepping towards Val. The big guy was falling back, terrified, as she lunged at his throat.

"Gaah," he screamed.

Then she swung around like Buffy the Vampire Slayer, sending a kick right into his groin.

Val bent over, holding his most delicate parts with both hands. "I give, I give!" he screamed.

McGoo was moaning on the ground.

And the Blob was running away as fast as his fat legs would carry him.

"How did you do that?" I asked as Rochelle extended a hand to lift me up.

"Karate," she replied, just a little out of breath, "five years, brown belt."

"Wow," I said, truly impressed.

"I really don't like being called a chink," Rochelle told the moaning McGoo. "My family is from Singapore, not the mainland."

Rochelle and I held hands as we left the two fallen guys. We talked briefly about laying charges and whether Rochelle might end up in more trouble than the guys would. In the end, it seemed best to forget about the whole thing. Still, there was a question hanging in the air.

"So what does the blond guy have against you?" Rochelle asked.

"Well, I, uh, I went out with his sister . . ."

"Another ex-girlfriend?" she laughed.

"Yeah, I guess."

"You really *are* experienced," she said appreciatively.

I smiled. I still had the taste of freshly mown grass in my mouth, but the stars in my eyes at this moment were only because of the smile on Rochelle's face. Those stars began to shine a little brighter when Rochelle suggested we go back to her place so I could get cleaned up.

When we reached Rochelle's house, she took me up to the bathroom—a real girly bathroom with more hairdryers and shampoos than I had ever seen collected in one place in my entire life. I stared at myself in the mirror. I had dirt on my chin, a cut on my mouth and a kind of grass moustache over my upper lip. A little soap and water took care of the dirt and grass. The cut required a little more attention.

"Sit on the edge of the tub," Rochelle told me.

I did as she ordered.

Rochelle went into the medicine cabinet and pulled out a bottle of disinfectant. She put a small amount on a cloth, then bent towards me.

"This might hurt."

"I'll be strong."

She smiled and touched the cloth to my cut lip. There was a brief flash of pain, but that wasn't my biggest sensation. What I felt the most was how erotic this was: a beautiful girl, bending over, touching my lips. It made no sense, of course. I had been insulted and beaten up, rescued and cleaned up . . . and now I was feeling horny.

"Maybe you should rest a little before we go out," Rochelle said.

"I'm fine, really, uh . . ."

"My room is just down the hall," she whispered.

"Oh, like, *rest* awhile. Well, yeah."

So I followed Rochelle down the hall until we reached the door to her bedroom. It was very, very cool. The bed and dresser were super modern, with wonky curves and handles; the walls were covered in French impressionist prints; the little stereo was a perfect silver Nakamichi; the computer was a slim Sony Vaio. The entire room was neat as a pin—except for a few dozen shoes scattered on the floor. Rochelle had to kick them aside as we came in.

I sat down on the bed, my heart beating like crazy. I hadn't been hurt very badly in the fight, but I felt I might have a coronary any second.

"I'll get another pillow so you can lean back," she said.

"Mmm," I said, as her hair brushed against my cheek.

"How do you feel?" she asked as I settled. Now I was lying on the bed and Rochelle was sitting on the edge, her body pressed right into me.

"Oh, I'm, uh . . ." At this point, speech was starting to be too much for me. A lot of blood was getting pumped into my body, but it wasn't going to my brain.

She brushed her hand against my forehead. "You feel a bit warm," she said.

"Mmm," I repeated.

"But look down here," she said with a smile. "There seems to be a sign of life."

And indeed there was.

"Let me see if I can help with that," Rochelle whispered, and then she pressed her lips against mine.

# 20

# Ah, Poetry

SOMEBODY SAID THAT falling in love is when Top 40 songs stop sounding silly and begin to sound like deep wisdom. The entire next day, I kept singing Top 40 songs, thinking about just how much extra meaning there was in each verse. I mean, Shania Twain was sounding real profound.

Was I in love?

"It's probably just lust," Jeremy responded. "You're such a horny guy and now you've finally got a girl who's willing to touch that disgusting body of yours. It's a miracle, but it's only lust."

Maybe I shouldn't have told him. Jeremy has such a piggish brain. He's watched too many porn films to have any idea what kind of emotions I was feeling.

I sighed. "You don't understand."

"Alan, when you've had as many girls as I've had, you won't go ga-ga after getting to second base. Love is love. Sex is sex. Don't confuse them." It was hard to believe all this wisdom coming from Jeremy, whose knowledge of philosophy was not nearly as good as his knowledge of history.

"I guess you're right," I said, "but I can't stop thinking about her. She smart, she's gorgeous, she's loving, she's . . . everything."

"Please, Al, I'm going to barf if you keep this up."

I did not keep it up. I realized that Jeremy was either crude or unsympathetic. What I really needed was another list from Maggie, but I thought that might lead to some embarrassing questions. Besides, Maggie's bills were already digging heavily into my bank account. I counted the words in Instruction Set 3, added on the coffee money, and figured her May billing was getting close to a hundred bucks already. I didn't know if I could *afford* any more advice.

Besides, I was doing quite well on my own. I was talking to Rochelle on the phone every night. She'd phone me or I'd phone her cell, and that was on top of all the instant messaging. She had fallen for me, or I had fallen for her, or we were both falling in the direction of real commitment. I mean, this was serious.

You'd think that during these earnest conversations I would have managed to reveal the truth about myself, little by little, but that was not the case. What actually happened is that I added more and more details to Al Macklin's college life. I made up stories about my Italian class, invented details about my supposed math-for-poets class, pretended I'd seen Rochelle on campus while staring out the window of my English lit. class.

I had constructed in my mind, and in hers, a brand-new me. The Al Macklin I made up was a serious student, interested in Romantic poetry, struggling through his other required first-year courses, desperate to move out of his parents' home and into a shared house like Rochelle's. I have to admit that the Al Macklin I made up was a lot more interesting than the Al Macklin I happened to be. Someday, I said to myself, I'll have to get my real life to match my imagination.

The next Thursday, Rochelle suggested that we go out again, this time to a coffee house at the student centre. Some local band was playing '20s New Orleans jazz, and that sounded pretty good to me. Besides, it would give me a chance to use my fake ID and maybe get both of us a little drunk. If I'd managed to get to second base pretty much sober, imagine how far I could get with a little booze to break down inhibitions. Booze, KFUG and patience—how could I lose?

"Hey you," she said when I met her on campus.

"Hey to you too," I replied. It was a routine we'd developed on the phone.

And then we kissed. She did this little fluttery thing with her tongue that just drove me wild.

"Can I have another one of those?" I asked.

"Later," she said, squeezing my hand.

*Yes! Later!* I said to myself. And then another voice came in. *Don't rush things. Love and sex follow their own timetable.* I really do pay attention to those memos from Maggie.

We got into the pub without having to show a student card, and my fake ID was enough, along with $12, to get us a pitcher of beer. Rochelle admitted that she didn't drink very much; after recent events, neither did I. Besides, I wanted to be ready for anything that night.

The pub wasn't very crowded, maybe because exams were on, so I talked to Rochelle about how hard I was studying. The Italian final, I told her, was going to be a killer, but I thought the English lit. would be a piece of cake. "I'm just hoping there's a question on Lord Byron," I said, using my new-found Internet knowledge. "I know *Don Juan* like the back of my hand."

Rochelle looked at me with these wonderfully approving eyes.

After a while the band came up on stage. They were mostly a bunch of old guys with their grey hair tied back in little ponytails, except for the trumpeter, who seemed about thirty. I thought I recognized one of the guys in the band, but I couldn't quite place him. The trumpeter, however, really was from New Orleans and had the drawl to prove it.

"He sounds like Louis Armstrong," Rochelle said.

"Yeah, definitely," I agreed. It occurred to me that I knew absolutely nothing about jazz. But Rochelle was running her bare foot up and down my leg, so my ignorance didn't seem that much of a problem.

So we listened and drank and looked into each other's eyes and all this was going very well until a bunch of kids came into the pub right after the first set. They were noisy and kind of stupid, so I turned to see what all the noise was about.

And there they were—about half the kids in my math class. Maggie, Scrooge, Nikki, Allison, Hannah the Honker and a half-dozen others.

There should be a word for the sudden rush of fear when something like that happens, a word like *kafoozle*, a word to capture that rush of panic and embarrassment and the need for instant reaction.

"Alan, you're sweating all of a sudden," Rochelle said.

"It's nothing," I lied. "Hot flashes, that's all. Just a little *kafoozle*."

She giggled, not that the word was all that funny. It's just that Rochelle giggles at all my lines, and in the most adorable way.

*Do I ignore those guys?* I asked myself. *Do I turn away and hide and pray that none of them sees me? Do I walk over and say hello and try to keep them away from Rochelle?*

While I was paralyzed, unable to decide what to do, Maggie and Scrooge made the choice for me. The two of them walked over to our table with grins on their faces.

"Alan, my man, glad to see you . . . but gladder to see your friend," Scrooge began. He had this enormous girl-killing grin on his face, as if he were going to steal Rochelle away by the force of his smile. "Hello, hello," he said to Rochelle, ignoring me for the time being. "My name's Leroy but everybody calls me Scrooge."

"Scrooge?" Rochelle asked.

"Yeah, it's a long story. I'd love to tell you about it sometime."

Maggie pulled him back. "Down, Scrooge. Down," she said, as if Scrooge were a slobbering dog.

"Aww," Scrooge whined.

"Just ignore him," Maggie told Rochelle. "He sees a pretty girl and he goes into this automatic obnoxious mode. Nice to see you again, Rachel," Maggie said, mangling her name just a little. Then Maggie turned to me. "I guess you came to see Mr. Greer with the group."

"Mr. Greer?" I said. No, that was stupid. Try to keep the conversation general, I told myself, and get them to go away. Somehow I've got to get them to go away.

"Yeah, our math teacher is playing the bass, can you believe it?" Scrooge told Rochelle. "We thought he only knew about irrational numbers. Guess he also knows some Dixieland numbers."

That was a groaner, and it got exactly that response.

"Is Mr. Greer a prof?" Rochelle asked.

"No, no," I said. "He's a high-school teacher. Trigonometry, that kind of thing."

"We're all in his class," Scrooge volunteered.

I shuddered. I sweated. I stuttered. "We . . . we . . . we *were* all in his class."

"Yeah, like yesterday," Scrooge went on, ignoring me.

Maggie just stared at me. Her eyes were always pretty big, and seemed even bigger after she ditched her glasses and got the contacts, but now her eyes were positively enormous. Enormous and staring at me.

"It, uh, feels like yesterday," I went on. "Doesn't it, Scrooge?" I said, glaring at him. I was giving him simultaneous thought transmission, beaming right into his brain: *Go along with this, you idiot, and I'll owe you big time, like forever.*

"Oh, yeah, yeah," Scrooge said, somehow getting it. "It was like, really, ages ago, but a guy like that is hard to forget, you know."

I breathed a quick sigh of relief, my eyes glazing over until Maggie came into focus.

"Just how long ago was it, Al?" Maggie asked. She had this strange smile on her face, as if she knew she were sticking a dagger into my gut.

"Oh, a couple years. You *remember* our trig class, don't you?" I was sweating like the proverbial pig; even my hand was shaking as I reached for my beer. *Please, Maggie,* I prayed, *please just let me keep my little fraud going. Please let me keep just a little shred of dignity.*

"Oh yes, I do," Maggie replied. "How could I forget?" She smiled a conspiratorial smile.

I let out my breath. She wasn't lying, but she wasn't exposing me either.

That's when Rochelle raised another delicate issue. "Alan tells me that you two used to go out."

"Well, I guess, in a way," Maggie said. "I guess you could say I taught him everything he knows about girls."

"Then I owe you," Rochelle said. "He's turned out to be quite a guy." She reached over and took my hand in this wonderful, loving way.

Maggie gave her a strange smile. "C'mon," she said to Scrooge, "I think these two really want to be alone. Besides, I'm feeling a pressing need to . . ." The rest of the sentence was mostly lost because the band started playing, but I have a hunch that it really concluded with the words "throw up."

I picked up a napkin and wiped my forehead, then cuddled beside Rochelle so the two of us could watch the stage. Mr. Greer was up there, plucking away at a big double bass, not looking at all like the guy who held the chalk in our math class.

"You know, Al," Rochelle whispered in my ear. "That girl Maggie still isn't over you."

"Oh?" I said.

"Yeah, girls can tell. I think seeing you here with me made her kind of jealous. She was definitely covering something up."

I was smart enough to say nothing. The jealous part was pretty silly, but the covering-up part was too close to the truth. Didn't Mark Twain say something about that? Better to keep your mouth shut and appear ignorant than to open it and remove all doubt. Besides, Rochelle was chewing gently on my ear so I was having some trouble concentrating.

Oh, it should have been a fine, fine night. It should have been the kind of night about which songs are written and poets dream. It should have been "Dover Beach" meets "You're Still the One."

Rochelle and I sat, hand in hand, arm around shoulder, touching, kissing, sighing, dreaming. Or at least she was sighing and dreaming. I was desperately trying to figure out my next move. What if Scrooge came over and spilled the beans? What if Maggie really was jealous and decided to tell Rochelle everything? What could I do? How could I possibly recover?

But while the band played, a miracle occurred. My high-school classmates slowly disappeared in the darkness. After the second set, Maggie was gone and Scrooge had gone off to put the moves on some blonde girl at another table. After the third set, not even Hannah the Honker remained. They were all gone by the time Rochelle and I made our way outside, and nowhere in sight as we made our way back to Rochelle's place.

Then the miracles continued. It was a warm, warm night and Rochelle's room doesn't have any air conditioning, so it kind of made sense to take off our shirts as we made out on her bed. And then it kind of made sense for her to take off a little more, since I was so busy running my hands up and down her back. And then maybe it made sense for us to throw the rest of our clothes into the pile we had already started on the floor.

Now if I were a poet, I could write something wonderful about a guy's very first contact with a woman, skin to skin, body to body. I could write something about the silken skin of the female, the roughness of a man's flesh, the way two bodies can intertwine in ways that are physical and more than physical, sexual and more than sexual. But I am not a poet, so I won't go on. But I will tell you about the most wonderful nine words I've ever heard, a kind of prose poem.

The words were from Rochelle. They were whispered.

"Let me show you this little thing I learned."

Ah, poetry!

# 21

# The Truth Will Out

"YOU GOT TO THIRD BASE!" Jeremy cried.

We were sitting in the cafeteria, right after the holiday weekend, so his announcement brought more than a few looks from the other kids. Naturally, I turned red.

"Would you just be quiet," I snapped at him.

"But, Alan, my man, you've had a triumph! I mean, the way you're going, you'll have her in the sack by the end of the week."

"Shhh," I said. "Listen, Rochelle and I have a . . . a relationship. This isn't just about sex. Besides, we haven't had sex yet. We just . . ."

"I know, I know, you're getting deeply serious and she's a wonderful girl and you respect her and all that. But, Alan, what is the point? The point is you getting laid. I mean, you're almost there."

Somehow I found Jeremy to be just too crude in his description. Rochelle and I had spent the rest of the night making out on her bed. But what I loved most was lying across from her, looking into her eyes, tracing her eyebrows with my fingers, kissing her again . . . and again. Sure, it was physical, but it was so much more.

"Jeez, you'd think you were in love," Jeremy said in disgust.

Was I in love? Was this it—the big one? When all you really want to do is be with someone, to look at someone, to dream about someone . . . is that love?

"Well, I dunno. I guess, maybe, kind of—" I could have gone on with a list of idiotic comments, but that's when Maggie appeared. I could see her bearing down on us from across the cafeteria, fire in her eyes. The look on her face brought me back to harsh reality.

"You—sleazebag!" she said, slamming into a chair beside Jeremy. The pause was actually filled with a couple of good curse words. I hadn't realized, before this, that Maggie could swear like a sailor.

"Well, I, uh—" My dialogue isn't even worth writing down.

"You are slime. You are scum. You are worse than scum. You are the deep unclean that defeats even Lysol. You are the scummiest of the scum!"

"Well, I, uh—"

"That girl *likes* you!" Maggie exclaimed. "That poor deluded girl actually thinks you are what you pretend! So what year in college did you tell her, Al? Are you a first year, second year, a Rhodes Scholar? How wild a story is it?" The words were literally dripping with disgust.

"I, uh, well . . ."

"You . . . you lying, dissembling con man. You somehow managed to convince Rochelle that you're a college student! You incredible fraud, you two-faced piece of filth!"

Every single person in the cafeteria was staring at us. Maggie stopped and became aware of the eyes that were turned in our direction. I sat there, open mouthed. And Jeremy began to applaud. Soon the applause spread through the cafeteria. Even the people who hadn't heard Maggie's speech knew that she'd said something heroic.

Maggie shook her head as the applause died down. Then, in a quieter voice, she added, "And I went along with it. I gave you *advice!*"

"Thank you," I said, my voice very quiet.

"I'm almost as much of a scum as you are. I betrayed another woman," she moaned.

"No, you stood by your friend in a moment of need," I suggested.

"We're both scum, but you are worse," Maggie said. Her eyes really did shoot fire at moments like this. I suspect it's her Scottish background, all the bagpipes and haggis in her blood. They are moralistic people, the Scots. I read that somewhere, and I could see it in Maggie.

"I'm going to tell her the truth," I said, looking at Maggie with as much sincerity as I could muster.

"Before or after you get her in the sack?" Maggie asked.

"Before," I mumbled. "For sure, before."

"Al's already at third base," Jeremy offered, helpfully.

"Third base?" Maggie asked.

"That's like, you know . . ." Jeremy kind of choked on the explanation.

"You're at *third base*?" Maggie repeated, her voice rising. "You lie to this girl and pretend that you're somebody you're not and you . . .?" Her voice was still rising, and people began looking at us again. "And you tell your stupid friend about it and you're proud about getting to third base and now you're thinking about a home run and all the while you're lying to this girl, you're—"

Maggie stopped. She looked around at the cafeteria, which was in a hushed silence, and then back at us.

"You're pathetic."

"I know," I said.

"Pathetic," she repeated.

This time there was only a smattering of applause. Still, we had obviously been lunchtime entertainment for half the school.

"Look on the bright side," Jeremy said. "At least Maggie hasn't called you a pervert."

"No," Maggie spat out. "I'll save that adjective for you."

Jeremy looked down at his hands. I'd never seen him turn red in the face before.

Maggie shook her head. She was in charge right now, and she knew it. "I'm tired of chewing you out in front of an audience, and I want some time to think." Then she went on in a quieter voice. "So listen up, I want to see both of you at Starbucks after school. We've got to talk."

I read somewhere that the phrase "we've got to talk" is the single most ominous thing a girl can say to a guy, or vice versa. Certainly the way Maggie said it implied a threat, maybe that she'd call Rochelle and tell her the truth or, maybe worse, that she'd tell everybody what I'd done. Or not done.

I mean, it wasn't that I'd *done* anything that awful. I'd seen a pretty girl, asked her out, gone on a date, made out at her house. Nothing special in all that. Any given day, any country on earth, that same story is happening a million times. It wasn't that I didn't care about Rochelle, or that I was only using her for my own needs. I mean, I loved her, kind of, maybe. Or at least I was in love, or something like that.

The only problem was what I *hadn't done*, that I hadn't admitted to being a high-school student. Okay, maybe it was more than that. Maybe I had said a few things to give the impression that I went to college.

Okay, admit it. I lied. I fabricated. I created the Alan Macklin that I'm going to be in a couple of years and I pretended that guy was *already* me. Is that so awful?

Yeah, it's probably that awful.

I wouldn't feel bad about lying to somebody like Mel Halvorsen, who didn't seem to care much about the difference between truth and falsehood herself. I wouldn't feel bad about lying to one of my teachers, because they expect it, really, as part of the job. But when you lie to somebody you care about, well, that's pretty low. And when you drag in your friends to lie on your behalf, well, that's even lower.

So I sat at Starbucks that afternoon and looked morosely into my grande cup. It's a good word, *morosely*, because it even sounds like how I felt. *Morosely.* Lots of really good words in that vocabulary book I've been studying.

"C'mon, Alan, cheer up," Jeremy said.

"Why?"

"What's the worst that can happen?" he said. "You should always think about it like that. The worst thing she can do is tell Rochelle the truth, and you were going to tell her the truth anyhow."

"Yeah, but it would be different coming from me. And she'll probably dump me after she finds out."

"There are a lot of fish in the sea," he said. "I know a dozen girls at St. Hilda's who are desperate enough to hop in the sack with you. And there's always Hannah the Honker."

"Rochelle is not a fish, Jeremy," I spat back. "But you are a jerk. A total jerk."

I might have gone on in that vein, but Maggie came in at the door and looked at the two of us. The look alone was enough to shut me up. In a few minutes she came over to our table with her double latte.

"Okay, I've been thinking," she began. Her face was serious, but not angry. When Maggie gets angry her face tightens up and her little red eyebrows push together over her nose. When she gets serious her mouth tightens up and her cheeks look like a chipmunk's. This was the chipmunk look.

"We can see," Jeremy said.

"It's time for the truth," Maggie went on. "Either you promise to tell Rochelle or else I will. She's got to know, Alan."

"Right. I'll tell her."

"Tonight or tomorrow. Promise?"

"Promise," I said. I was ready to cross my heart, but I thought that might be over the top.

"If she really cares about you, maybe she'll understand."

"Right," I agreed. I try to tell myself this was true, but all the while my heart was sinking.

That's when Jeremy decided to join the conversation, in his usual way. "Maybe she'll take pity on you, Al. You might get to home base yet."

Maggie stared at him. "Has it occurred to you, Jeremy, that your obsession with sex is a serious personal problem, verging on pathological in your case?"

"What, me?" he replied.

"Yeah, you," Maggie shot back. "First base, second base, home run—you'd think that a relationship was a game where you keep score: guys over girls 9 to 4 in the fifth. It's no wonder nobody will go out with you."

"What do you mean?" Jeremy asked.

"I mean, you've never even been out with a girl—"

"C'mon, I've been out with lots of girls. I've already run all the bases. I mean, like . . ."

"That's a crock," Maggie told him. "Not one girl at our school has ever been out with you, nor would they, given your reputation as a perv. And those girls at St. Hilda's you talk about, that's all fantasy. Who was that last girl you talked about, Britney something? Well, I asked a friend over there and she says there is no girl with that name. In fact, she says that no girl at St. Hilda's has ever even heard of you."

Jeremy was visibly shrinking in his seat as we both stared at him.

"Yeah, well, you can't always believe everything—"

"Frankly, I'd believe my friends over a slimebag like you," Maggie told him. "There's nothing that says a guy has to go out. God knows, I'd never been on a date until this year, and that's the simple truth. But when you make up big stories about your imaginary sexual conquests and it's all fantasy, well, that's sick."

Jeremy's face was very pale, as if all the blood in his body had rushed somewhere else. He looked like a corpse.

"If all your fantasies weren't fired up by porn movies, maybe it wouldn't be so bad. Maybe the only one affected would be you," Maggie said. "But now the fraud is getting contagious, so," she turned back to me, "it stops tonight."

"Tomorrow," I croaked. "I'll tell her tomorrow."

"Fair enough," Maggie replied. "Better that she hears it from you. 'The truth will out,' Alan, remember that."

"Yeah, right," I said. "Definitely."

"And one more thing," Maggie said, reaching into her notebook. "Here's your final bill. I can't keep giving advice to a client who isn't honest about what he's doing," she said, and slapped the envelope on the table. "I quit."

# 22

# Some Truths Are Surprising

THE TRUTH WILL OUT. Sounds like Shakespeare. That's the kind of thing he used to write. *Out, out, damned spot,* and all that stuff. Someday I have to read more Shakespeare. Maybe if I really were a college English lit. major I'd know all sorts of Shakespeare and could start spouting all sorts of wonderful quotes.

But I'm not. I'm a miserable high-school student who's lied to the one girl who really likes me. I have deceived and taken advantage of the one girl I have ever loved, or kind of loved, or at least liked a lot. And I lied to the one person who was giving me really good advice.

I am scum. I am worse than that. I am high-school scum.

My only solace is that Jeremy is worse than me. He did lie—he lied to me, his best friend. And even when Maggie made it obvious, he still kept trying to cover it up. On the way home, he started coming up with even mangier lies—like maybe he mixed up St. Hilda's and St. Clement's, or maybe the girls he went out with were so upset when he dumped them that they lied to Maggie.

"Sure," I said. We both knew that he was still trying to keep his cover, and how pathetic that was, so there seemed no sense rubbing it in.

But lying to your best friend is really low, about as low as you can go. And when I thought back to all the dumb advice he'd given me about girls, KFUG and all that, it made me cringe. I'm too trusting, I told myself. I have to learn how to separate the truth from the lies, and I might as well start with Rochelle and me. It was time to bite that bullet.

"Rochelle, I've got to see you tonight," I said into her cellphone message box Saturday morning. "Is there any way?"

I had to beat my mother to the phone when she called back about an hour later. Rochelle had an exam that went to seven o'clock, but said we could go out for dinner after that. She said she really wanted to see me, too.

My hand was shaking when I hung up the phone. That girl was so lovely, so kind, so loving . . . how could I have been such a jerk? She thought I was just desperate to see her because I felt so strongly about her—and I did—but now I've got to deliver a little stunner. Uh, sorry, I'm not the Alan you thought I was. I'm just a miserable high-school student—a miserable, deceiving high-school student.

Maybe, just maybe, she'd forgive me. That's what I told myself. And then I remembered that it was Jeremy who had given me that hopeful scenario, and what did he know? Nothing. The truth was simple—I was toast. Worse, I was burnt toast stinking up the kitchen.

We met outside the room where she wrote her exam.

"Alan, you look so serious," Rochelle said.

"Yeah, well, it's been a rough couple of days," I said with a sigh. "Studying for exams, you know." *No, stop that,* I told myself. *You've got to stop that.*

"It's always like that at the end of the term," she replied.

I cringed. I should tell her. I should blurt out the truth, but I just couldn't—not there, not with all her classmates looking at us.

"So let's go have something to eat," she said. "This is my last exam, so it's time to celebrate. And I've got something kind of serious to talk to you about."

"Me too." Another sigh. "What kind of food?"

"Anything except Chinese," she said. "Italian's my fave. There's a little place not too far away called Vincenzo's or something like that. Might as well have a nice dinner before a serious talk."

It shouldn't have surprised me that there was a little awkward distance between us that night. We talked about nothing much on the way to the restaurant, and didn't even hold hands or kiss. It was as if she already had a hunch what I was going to say.

Vincenzo's turned out to be a nicer place than I had expected, not so much a pizza parlour as a decent Italian restaurant with a couple of things beside pizza on the menu. I said that the meal would be my treat. It seemed unfair that I should be dumping the truth on her if she was picking up the bill. And maybe, just maybe, she'd take pity on me if I were buying the dinner.

So we ate lasagna, drank some wine and talked about school and life and this universe or its alternatives, carefully avoiding anything *important* for maybe an hour.

I was good. I did not add to any of the lies I had previously told. I merely dodged sideways when she asked about Professor Jones, or my art history course, or why I couldn't handle the menu when I had spent the whole year studying Italian. I would smile, be charming, and say nothing.

The wine didn't help. The more I drank, the more beautiful and sweet and loving Rochelle became. I found myself staring into her eyes like some kind of lovesick puppy. And maybe I was in love. Maybe the love I felt had gotten that much stronger because it was doomed, because my little bombshell of truth would leave our relationship lying in pieces all over the battlefield.

"Chelle," I said when the cappuccinos arrived, "I've got to tell you something."

"Me too," she said, looking into my eyes over the edge of her coffee cup.

"It's hard because I really like you," I began. "I mean, I really, really like you. You're the most wonderful, most beautiful . . . and I don't mean just beautiful but . . ."

"You're making me blush."

"Well, I'm saying that when we're together, it's so special."

"Alan." My name just hung in the air, the tone of her voice carrying so much feeling, so much sheer devotion, or fondness, or maybe love. "Alan, I know how you feel. I've felt the same way, since that first night."

I had to get this back on track. I had to tell her the truth. Somehow.

"But the truth is," she went on, "that we're both pretty young."

I raised one eyebrow. Did she know? Had Maggie called her?

"What I mean is," Rochelle said, looking away from me, "this relationship we have is getting pretty intense, pretty fast."

I nodded. That was true, very true.

"And I'm not sure I'm quite ready for that," Rochelle said. "You're pretty experienced with girls, but I've only had one boyfriend before you and . . . well . . . there's something else."

I put down my cappuccino cup. It was empty.

Rochelle looked upset.

"After we . . . the other night, well, you know, I got all confused. I want this relationship with you, really I do, but I got kind of scared because it was so . . . so soon. And I haven't been entirely honest with you because, well, there's this other guy . . ."

"Another guy," I repeated like a zombie. "There's another guy?"

"Well, it's so weird, Alan. I mean, with you there's this big physical thing. I can't believe how I feel when I'm with you, but with him it's so different."

"With this other guy," I repeated. I could feel the anger rising up out of my chest and into my head; I could feel my thyroid or pituitary or whatever gland it is pumping anger molecules into my bloodstream. I was jealous. I was hurt. I was mad.

"It's more kind of spiritual, you know," she went on. "Not that what we have isn't spiritual, but there's this big attraction . . ."

"And you like this other guy better," I said.

She shook her head. "No, not better. It's not like that. You're both so very different. You're so experienced, so confident, and he's a bit younger and . . ."

"What's his name?" I demanded.

"Alan, don't," she pleaded.

"What's his name?" I repeated. "If you're going to dump me, I want to know the guy's name. It's only fair, Rochelle."

She thought for a second, maybe trying to decide if I were the violent type that would go over to the guy's house with an Uzi. Ultimately, I guess she figured that wasn't my style.

Here eyes were so apologetic as his name came from her lips.

"Braden," she whispered. "Braden Boyce."

# 23

# When All The Birds Do Squawk

IT WASN'T FAIR, any of it. I'd only been in love for a week. I'd only been seeing Rochelle for a month and now I was . . . dumped.

This whole business of love and loss is really quite physical. When you're in love, your heart beats wildly, you stand straighter, you smile more, you hear all the sweet birds sing. When you're dumped, your heart relocates into your stomach, you walk with a stoop, you can't remember what a smile looks like and all the birds begin to squawk.

The next day, I lay in bed. I told my mother I was sick and just lay in bed. In some other century, in the words of some romantic poet, I would be *languishing* for loss of my beloved. That's a nice word, *languish*. It kind of sounds how I felt. I languished in front of *The New Price Is Right, Days of Our Lives*, a cooking show and Jerry Springer, interspersed with bits of the Discovery Channel. I knew I was terribly, terribly sad when *Days of Our Lives* started to feel like my real life, and the guests on Jerry Springer started to look like comparatively sensible people.

The phone rang at four. I could tell by the call display that it was Jeremy.

"How are you, guy?" he asked.

"Languishing," I said. "I've been dumped. I have no reason to live."

"Bummer," he replied. That's about as much sympathy as guys give each other. "But she's only a girl, Al," he went on. "You'll get over it."

"How would you know?" I shot back, then thumped down the phone.

I didn't eat supper that night. My mother was convinced that I should go see Dr. Signurdson, but I maintained that my particular malady couldn't be fixed by an antibiotic. I was in despair; I was cultivating melancholy. Somebody wrote a book about that once, *Anatomy of Melancholy*, just in case you wanted to dissect the emotion. I didn't. I wanted to wallow in it.

On Saturday, the phone rang again. This time it was Maggie, so I picked up.

"We've both been dumped," she began.

I sighed. "I know."

"Those two-timers were seeing each other behind our backs."

"Must have been."

"Scum, they're both scum."

"Well, Braden is," I agreed. "Rochelle, well, Rochelle, I think, well . . ."

"Al, you were taken in," Maggie said. "You fell big time and she just played with you. She *used* you."

"I guess."

"So stop moaning about it and get angry," she told me. "You don't see me moaning over Braden Boyce. No way. The guy wanted to get laid, and when I wouldn't oblige him he looked elsewhere. I mean, what kind of guy is that?"

I figured that was a rhetorical question, so said nothing.

"A scum," Maggie said, answering her own question. "But enough of that. Rochelle and Braden are ancient history. For current history, we've got a project on the role of women in World War II and it's due next week."

"We do?" I croaked.

"Yeah, I signed you up on Friday. I figured since you're not a client any more we could probably do a project together. I thought we could do a PowerPoint show and dazzle the class. How about we get together tomorrow and do the research?"

"But I'm languishing," I replied.

"Yeah, like Ophelia for Hamlet, and look where it got her—floating down a stream clutching a bunch of flowers. It's time to move on, Al."

"Okay," I groaned. "Your place or mine?"

"Pretty funny, Al. You've got a high-speed connection, haven't you?"

"Yeah."

"So let's get together at your place," she said. "And I don't mean to bug you about this, Al, but could I get that final bill paid? It *is* the end of May, you know."


The final bill wasn't all that bad: $20 for consulting time, $26 for Instruction Set 3, $38 for expenses for a total of $84. There was the guarantee, of course, which I could have used—after all, the Ultimate Goal hadn't been achieved. But given all the work that Maggie had put into my project, I figured she deserved the money, and probably a lot more.

So I had the last payment ready when Maggie came pounding on the door of my house on Sunday afternoon. My mother was out, fortunately, or else she would have cookied poor Maggie to death. My father looked at Maggie with a question in his eyes, as if to say, *So is this why I gave you those condoms?* Which might be why I told him that Maggie was "a friend, just a friend."

Maggie seemed to take my father's inspection quite well, shaking his hand in a businesslike way and giving both of us a big smile. In fact, Maggie's smile was so big that I'd forgotten she used to wear braces. Then I noticed that her eyes were quite large and quite blue, and actually quite attractive as eyes go.

But what really stopped me cold was Maggie's outfit. Instead of her standard school outfit of baggy-everything, she was wearing a little miniskirt and some kind of tight top. I tried not to stare, but from the corner of my eye I could see that Maggie actually had a drool-worthy shape. Following her into our computer/TV/everything room, watching her butt as it moved under the skirt, I came to a remarkable conclusion.

Maggie is a babe!

Of course, Maggie was also my friend and former dating adviser, so I really shouldn't have been noticing. We were doing a project, that's all. Homework, that's all. And I was heartbroken— languishing—so I really shouldn't be paying attention to women, any women.

Together, we worked on the project. Maggie is a spread-it-out-on-the-floor kind of organizer while I'm a type-it-on-the-computer kind of guy. Between the two systems, a pretty nifty PowerPoint show came together with lots of decent history, some cool images and an animated graphic or two. One advantage of having a real smart partner on a project is that you're almost guaranteed an A. On this one, I could see an A+, the kind of mark I sorely needed in history.

Near the end of the afternoon Maggie stopped being all business. The project was nearly finished, the sun was a golden orb outside the window, and Maggie was sitting on the floor in the pool of light that poured through the blinds.

"Al, do you think it was my skin?" she asked.

"What?" I said, clueless.

"My skin," she repeated. "I've got this awful freckle-skin. It's all blotchy and disgusting. Is that why Braden dumped me? Is Rochelle's skin nicer than mine?"

"I don't think guys notice skin that much," I said matter-of-factly. "Besides, your skin is nice, freckles or no freckles." That observation was true, really. Maggie didn't have too many zits or anything that terrible, she just had freckles. Redheads have freckles, that's all.

"So is it as nice as Rochelle's?" she asked.

"Absolutely," I said. I had a hunch that Maggie didn't need a detailed analysis of skin surface; she needed some ego-boosting.

"So what is it?" she asked. "Maybe I'm a bad kisser. You know, I really don't know that much about kissing."

"But you gave me all those instructions," I said.

"Yeah, but it's not like I've kissed a dozen guys. Most of what I wrote you I got out of *Cosmopolitan*. I've only had two boyfriends."

"Really?" I said, raising my eyebrows. "The way you talked . . ."

"Well, I guess I didn't want to seem stupid." She looked away from me. "I mean, that's why I needed all that advice from Allison and Hannah when you were getting close to third base with Rochelle. I've never gone that far."

"Hannah the Honker?" I said, amazed.

"Oh, you'd be surprised, Al."

"I just figured that somebody like you would have lots of guys going after you . . ."

Then we stopped talking and just looked at each other. In some other room, my father was playing an ancient disk of "Love Me Tender." A yellow stream of sunlight came beaming in the window at the two of us. One of Maggie's legs was up against mine, and our faces, at that moment, were almost touching.

"Maggie," I said, "there's a way we could answer your question. The one about kissing."

"Yeah?" she said.

"We could . . ."

Then I leaned my face into hers, and she tilted her head back a little, and our lips touched. We could have ended it right there. In fact, I was half expecting Maggie to push me away or even hit me.

But she didn't. She opened her lips and put her arms around my back, pulling me to her. So I put my arms around her, then began playing with her lips and her tongue with my tongue—gently, oh so gently—just as Maggie had instructed.

"Oh my god," I said when we came up for air. "You are such a good kisser."

"So are you," she replied. She sounded surprised, either at me or the kissing or herself. Maybe that's why she pushed me back and quickly got up off the floor.

In a minute she had dusted herself off, cleared her throat and gotten back that Maggie McPherson Consulting voice I knew so well. "Looks like Rochelle and Braden will never know what they're missing."

"Yeah, I guess not," I said.

"But business is business, Al, and if you can afford a little more advice . . ."

"Yeah, I can," I told her.

"Well, when you started going out with Rochelle I had another girl in mind for you. I had already done all the preliminary work. I had you all set up for a blind date."

"Really?"

"Yeah, so when you get over languishing," she went on, "I guess I could set something up for you. Usual fees, of course."

"I thought you quit as my adviser."

"I did," Maggie said. "But let's see if this girl works out and we can renegotiate something."

# 24

# Outside the Fee Schedule

IT'S AMAZING HOW quickly a guy can get over languishing when the prospect of another girl comes up. It's like in *Romeo and Juliet*, the way Romeo forgets all about Rosalind after Act I. So when my two days of languishing were finished, I found myself standing nervously on a downtown corner, the last Friday in May, holding flowers in my sweaty left hand.

I felt like a guy from the dating shows on television, the ones where some snide guy sits in a limo while the poor contestant stands waiting for his date, holding a bouquet that gets a cartoon label: *cheap flowers bought at corner store*.

Okay, maybe they were cheap, but they were still flowers. When I told Jeremy about this, he said that only a wuss would bring flowers for a blind date. But Jeremy's advice, I realize, is based on years and years of inexperience. I'm better left to my own devices, as somebody once said, maybe Keats or Shelley. Besides, instruction set number three said that girls like little gifts. Might as well start this the best way I know.

It was ten minutes after eight on my watch. The girl was supposed to meet me here, at this corner, right at eight o'clock, so maybe I was being stood up. The flowers felt more and more ridiculous as I waited, and people walked by looking at me with vague smirks on their faces. I was ready to give up when the door to the apartment building opened and Maggie came out.

"What happened?" I asked her. "The girl didn't show up?"

"No, your blind date is here," she said matter-of-factly.

"Like where?"

"Here," she repeated. "Right here. *I'm* your blind date, you idiot. How long does it take you to figure these things out?"

"You?"

"Me. So what do you think?"

Maggie stepped back so I could get a good look at her. She was dressed in a short, short skirt that made her legs look terrifically long, she wore a top that showed everything she usually kept hidden under a sweatshirt, and her hair actually sparkled as if it were dusted with jewels.

"Cool!" I said. So much for pretending I could put two words together to make a real sentence.

"Thank you," Maggie replied, blushing just a little from all my staring. "And thank you for the flowers, Alan. They're lovely."

Right. I had flowers in my hand. I was so busy staring that I'd forgotten all about them.

"Just remember the instructions, Al. Keep your eyes up."

"Right, eyes on eyes."

"Lay on the praise."

"You look great," I said. "You are great."

"You've learned a lot," Maggie said, taking my hand. "I got us tickets to a concert; the Foosballs are playing at the Phoenix."

"Oh, the Foosballs," I said, a little stunned. "One of my favourite groups." This was a lie, of course. I'd never even heard of the Foosballs and I could tell from Maggie's glance that she saw right through me. Still, it was a date, a real date, with a girl more glorious than I could possibly have imagined a few months ago.

"Here, you can study this while we wait for the bus." Then she handed me a neatly folded piece of paper.

## PROJECT: ALAN
Instruction set 4

Your goal tonight is to help create a wonderful date. The good news for you is that you're only responsible for half of it; the other half is my job. The bad news is that you *are* responsible for half of it, so try not to be too klutzy or clueless.

### Do's
1. Look at my eyes. Keep your eyes up there, buddy.
2. Use sucky phrases like "Gosh, that's a really interesting idea," or "How do you keep your hair so perfect all the time?" I rather like compliments: authentic ones are best, but inauthentic ones will do.
3. Be funny. You really are an amusing guy, so don't freeze up.
4. Be confident. You've had a lot of experience with girls now, so there's no reason to be timid.
5. Stick to your immediate goal. You want to make this date a success so there's a date two, date three, date four, etc. I know your real goal is the et cetera, but there's no timetable on that. Be patient. Await further instructions.

### Don'ts
1. Don't rush me. I'm a little nervous about all this, so give me the time I need.
2. Don't kiss me again until I really want to kiss you. You'll have to use intuition to determine the moment.
3. Don't feel or fondle any more than I let you.
4. Don't forget that no means no; so do unh-unh, nah, nix, and stop it right now. On the other hand, yes does mean yes. You can figure out the synonyms for yes by yourself.
5. Don't give up. I really do like you, Al. But I'm a bit confused by all this, so don't quit even if I mess up my end of things.

Need I mention that we had a wonderful time? The Foosballs really were pretty good. There was dancing and coloured lights and lots of cuddling together at the club. I really do like Maggie—I've *always* liked Maggie—except now it was different.

"You know what?" I said when we got back to her apartment building. We were kissing. In fact, we'd been doing a lot of kissing at the club, and in the taxi.

"What?"

"I think I'm falling in love."

"In love or in lust?" she asked, though the lust part had been pretty obvious.

"In love," I said, "seriously."

"Oh my," Maggie sighed.

"So now what do we do?" I asked.

"Kiss me goodnight," she replied, "and await further instructions. I just need to figure out what they are."

# About the Author

PAUL KROPP is the author of more than fifty novels for young people. His work includes six award-winning young adult novels, many books for reluctant readers, and four illustrated books for beginning readers. He also writes non-fiction books and articles for parents, and is a popular speaker on issues related to reading and education.